THE LAIRD'S ANGEL

CAROLINE LEE

COPYRIGHT

Copyright © 2020, Caroline Lee
Caroline@CarolineLeeRomance.com

ALL RIGHTS RESERVED. This book contains material protected under International and Federal Copyright Laws and Treaties. Any unauthorized reprint or use of this material is prohibited. No part of this book may be reproduced or transmitted in any form or by any means, electronic or mechanical, including photocopying, recording, or by any information storage and retrieval system without express written permission from the author.

First edition: 2020

This work is made available in e-book format by Amazon Kindle at www.amazon.com

Printing/manufacturing information for this book may be found on the last page

Cover: EDHGraphics

DEDICATION

*For those who are the heart of the team,
while keeping their own heart safe.*

∽

PROLOGUE

*L*ady Melisandre Lamond held her forgotten embroidery in her lap and watched the Queen of Scotland pace. She wondered if it was time to commission a new woven rug for the small solar; with the way Queen Elizabeth was wearing a track from one window to the opposite wall, they'd need one soon.

This room was considerably more intimate than the Queen's solar, which is why she'd given it over to her good friend, Charlotte Bruce, who was in command of the Queen's Angels. Charlotte's desk took up a good quarter of the space, leaving just enough room for her gathered Angels and the agitated Queen.

Well, not *all* of her Angels.

Mellie glanced across the room to the window seat, where her own dear friend, Rosalind, sat frowning at the view. She had one of her precious books open on her lap, but was making no attempt to turn the pages or even pretend she was reading, and Mellie wondered at that.

Was Rosa worried about Courtney?

The third member of their trio had left earlier that day

with one of the Queen's former guards, and Rosa already missed her presence as much as Mellie did. They each had their strengths, but when it came to action and battles, Court was the one they depended on to lead them.

And everyone in the room was very much afraid they may need her before she could return.

"In my own throne room," the Queen muttered again, turning away from the wall and beginning her journey back. "I cannot believe it."

"Believe it," Charlotte said in a bland voice, not looking up from her letter. Her stylus scratched against the parchment, the only sound, other than the swish of the Queen's skirts. "I've told ye time and again, Yer Majesty, ye need better security."

"Yes, and I am beginning to agree with you. I thought *surely*, with so many guards and my ladies around—"

Charlotte glanced up long enough to cock a brow at her friend. "Yer primary guards were still asleep when ye decided to meet with the Fraser delegation, remember?" And Charlotte ought to know; she was married to Liam Bruce, the head of the Queen's guards, who was one of the aforementioned slumbering guards. "Thank God my Angels arrived in time."

When she nodded to Mellie and Rosa, the Queen glanced their way.

"Yes," she murmured, turning once more and squeezing her hands into fists. "Thank God."

They nearly hadn't.

Mellie, Court and Rosa had been in Aboyne, interrogating a group of Grant warriors about the Fraser delegation's intentions. What they'd learned had sent them rushing back to Scone, hoping to arrive before the Queen met with the Fraser laird, a man the Grants had accused of being a traitor.

Court had sent Mellie and Rosa to the Queen's side to protect her, but when the threat materialized, neither had yet been close enough to help. It was only Court and her incredible skill with a bow, along with some help from Ross Fraser —the same former Queen's guard who was on a mission with Court now—who was able to react in time to take down the assassin, just before he reached the Queen.

It had been a hell of a way to start the morning.

Before he'd died, the assassin had only had time to respond to the question of who had sent him: saying only "Fraser." Damning enough, perhaps, but Court had also recognized the sign he gave as identifying him as a member of the Red Hand, a cutthroat gang of thieves and murderers who had raised her.

Court and Ross Fraser—who was still a suspect, as far as Mellie was concerned—had left earlier that day on their way to track down the Red Hand. If Court's old friend was still in command, they might have some luck determining why the gang was behind this assassination attempt.

If not, then Court might be in real danger.

As for the rest of them…

"One of us will always be at yer side, Yer Majesty," Mellie assured her. "Ye cannae be alone, not until this mystery is solved. Whoever sent that assassin will likely try again, since the first attempt failed."

The Queen glanced at Charlotte, who sighed and tossed the stylus down as she shook her head. The spy-mistress pressed her fingertips to her temples.

"Nay, Mellie," she finally said, "ye and Rosa arenae guards."

Mellie glanced at her teammate, who was still staring out the window. "I ken it well, Charlotte, but the Queen—"

"The Queen will be guarded," Charlotte snapped, finally meeting Mellie's eyes. She seemed to quickly regret her tone, because she sighed again and dropped her hands to her very pregnant belly. "My apologies."

Mellie lifted one shoulder in a shrug. "We're all on edge."

"Aye," Charlotte agreed with a grimace, exchanging a hooded look with the Queen, her best friend. "And the bairn isnae helping matters."

"How much longer?" Queen Elizabeth asked in a quiet voice.

It was Rosa who answered, still not looking their way. "Ten days, based on my calculations of Charlotte's cycle and the calendar. But she might labor early, as it is her first child."

Mellie's lips twitched, and she lifted her embroidery once more, hoping to cover her smile before her friend noticed. Leave it to Rosalind to have calculated something as intimate as Charlotte's fertility and due date, and then not even realize how odd it was to casually announce such a thing.

Still, the youngest Angel was brilliant, and as Charlotte often said, Rosa's mind was their best weapon. Mellie would never let her friend know she thought she was a bit strange.

"Ten days," Charlotte repeated to Elizabeth, somehow keeping a straight face. "Maybe sooner."

The Queen shook her head, hiding her own smile. "It's amazing you can know such a thing, Rosalind, when the midwives can merely guess."

Shrugging, Rosa finally turned from her study of the view and met the Queen's gaze. " 'Tis no' so difficult. The midwives just do no' like to be wrong."

"And *you* do not mind?" the Queen asked, with a raised brow.

"I am no' wrong."

Their youngest member said it with such confidence, the Queen had to turn away, but not before Mellie saw her smile bloom in full, knowing she should be thankful to Rosa for lightening the Queen's mood, but also knowing her fellow

Angel wouldn't understand why her odd claims would cause such a thing.

To ensure her friend wasn't hurt, Mellie tossed a smile her way, even as she focused her gaze on the tiny leaf she was embroidering around a pink rose. "Rosa's calculations have saved me a time or two."

Charlotte grunted in agreement, even as Rosa smirked and closed the book in her lap.

"Aye. Ye might no' be the *only* pregnant Angel around here, Charlotte, had I not taught Mellie to count very carefully."

The Queen's startled laughter was good to hear and caused them all to relax. Mellie shot her friend a grateful smile, forgiving Rosa for her teasing. And she was right; in Mellie's work, she had to keep careful count of the days to ensure she wouldn't fall pregnant inopportunely.

Once was more than enough.

Mayhap there was a flicker of that thought in Mellie's eyes, because Rosa suddenly winced, as if remembering Mellie's history. Her expression turned apologetic, but Mellie merely shook her head, just slightly, to let her friend know all was forgiven.

Bon Dieu!

Mellie teased Rosa often enough; she should be free to tease in return.

Unaware of the undercurrent between the friends, the Queen sighed and sank into a chair beside Charlotte's desk, finally relaxing with a smile. "When Robert's home, I do not even bother with the counting."

"When Robert's home, Yer Majesty," Charlotte teased with a wink, "I doubt ye have enough *time* to count."

All four women chuckled at the reference to the royal couple's tendency to "retire early" when they were together. But with the King so oft in Ireland, or traveling about the country, it was no wonder they took advantage of their time together.

And besides, the two of them—and all of Scotland—were desperate for another healthy pregnancy...of the male variety.

"Why do ye think he attacked me?" Elizabeth asked abruptly.

Mellie was startled enough by the change in topics, she pricked herself and dropped her embroidery to her lap once more with a muttered, "*Merde.*"

Lifting her finger to her lips, she glanced at Charlotte, who was frowning down at her papers once more.

"I donae ken," their leader said with a sigh. "Threats against the Bruce are logical, at least, but his Queen?"

"The royal succession," Rosa said matter-of-factly, and when they all turned to her, she shrugged. "It's obvious. Elizabeth has been pregnant enough to assure the kingdom she's fertile, but only two daughters have survived thus far."

Mellie winced at her friend's bluntness, but Elizabeth nodded thoughtfully.

"I would not trade dear Margaret nor Maude for the world, but I would be a fool not to feel the pressure of needing a royal heir."

"Now that Edward's dead, and without a legitimate son," Charlotte said, referring to the King's only remaining brother, "there's no clear heir, and that does present a worry for many people."

The Queen sighed. "You think I am not aware of this? Why do you believe Robert and I spend so much time abed?"

Mellie pulled her finger from her mouth and snorted. "If ye truly need to ask that, the King's doing something wrong."

All three women chuckled, as Mellie had intended. She had a role in the Angels, and she played it well.

"There's always Alex," Charlotte offered. "Although his mother seems to care little for politics."

Rosa shook her head. "His youth and illegitimacy would make for a nasty battle for the throne."

While Queen Elizabeth had been a prisoner in England for so many years, King Robert's legacy had been in jeopardy. So he'd declared his brother Edward his heir, and Edward's sons after him. Edward had been betrothed to Isabel de Strathbogie, as good as married in the eyes of many. But when he turned away from her to marry another, leaving her with sweet little Alex, she was devastated.

Mellie's hands tightened around the cloth in her lap.

This world they lived in seemed to be formed to allow men to do as they pleased to women—even sisters of powerful lairds—without consequence.

She should know.

Of course, Isabel had not been thrown to the wolves, the way Mellie had. Robert and his family made their support of Isabel's son clear, and now that Edward was gone, without legitimate heirs, Alex was the Crown's only hope, despite his bastardy.

Aye, by taking Isabel under her wing, Elizabeth had saved her. The same as she'd done for Mellie five years before.

Charlotte cleared her throat. "The point is moot, because Alex will *no'* become King of Scotland, aye?" She pierced each of her Angels with a glare. "The Bruce is hale and hearty, and Elizabeth will bear a son soon enough."

Understanding what Charlotte was after, Mellie nodded enthusiastically. "Aye, of course. The King will be home soon, and ye can practice some more. Surely there are positions to increase the hope of breeding?" She winked lewdly at the Queen. "I'll be happy to help research."

As expected, the Queen rolled her eyes with an indulgent smile. "I believe we can manage on our own, thank you."

"Whatever the future holds, we were discussing the assassin's motives," Rosa reminded them. "I believe my answer is still the strongest: With Elizabeth dead, the King would be free to marry again. A different wife—mayhap one with a son already?—would set many at ease when it comes to the royal succession."

"Marry again?" Mellie repeated. "Ye cannae think the King was behind—"

"Nay," Rosa was quick to assure them. "But mayhap someone with a sister or daughter available for the position? Ye ken, *nullum magnum ingenium sine mixtura dementiae fuit.*"

Ignoring Rosa's habit of spouting gibberish, Charlotte spat out, " 'Tis ridiculous! Why murder the Queen for such a weak reason? As if one woman is a better breeder than another?" Her hands dropped to her stomach. "If that is indeed the motive, I believe our mastermind to be a clotheid!"

Rosa shrugged, turning the book over in her hands, but not opening it again. "Then mayhap 'tis someone who already believes he has a valid claim to the throne."

Mellie's thoughts flashed to Isabel de Strathbogie, a woman who'd already borne a royal bastard—a male child. But the Queen trusted her, and the dear woman clearly wanted only to raise her son to steward the lands King Robert had gifted him upon his birth.

It was Elizabeth who shook them all, when she lifted her head to meet Charlotte's eyes. "If that is the case, then this person would have plans to harm Robert as well."

Charlotte's eyes widened on a whispered curse, and her gaze flew to Rosa's in question. The youngest woman shrugged once more.

"I cannae divine the future, Charlotte, but can only guess at the likely paths. If there's a man out there who believes he has claim to the throne, then killing Elizabeth before she bares a son, and getting rid of Robert soon after... Well, that would be a masterful strategy."

" 'Getting rid of?' " Elizabeth repeated with a shudder.

Mellie lifted her finger to her mouth once more, but this time to chew on a fingernail, a nervous habit leftover from childhood. When she realized she was doing it, she didn't bother stopping; these women were her friends, and she only allowed her bad habits to show around friends.

Charlotte reached for a new piece of vellum. "I will alert the King's guards. I'm sure he's heard about yesterday's attack already, but he needs to ken about our theory as well."

"Wait," Elizabeth commanded. "First, let us determine some suspects."

"It cannae be a coincidence the attack came during the Fraser's audience," Mellie offered, finally dropping her hand to her lap.

Charlotte scoffed. " 'Twould be foolhardy of the laird to link himself so boldly to an attack."

"Unless he guessed us to come to such a conclusion," Rosa pointed out.

"If the Fraser of Lovat *guessed* at any of this..." The Queen's words trailed off as she gestured around the small room to the Angels and her spy-mistress, then shook her head. "We would be in danger indeed."

"I doubt he did, Yer Majesty."

"Aye," Mellie agreed with Rosa. "There's nae way a man like Lachlan Fraser would suspect us—*any* of us—to be more than pretty faces."

The Queen hummed skeptically. "Pretty faces?"

With a lewd smile, Mellie lifted her hands to cup her breasts. "I doubt he was looking at my *face*, Yer Majesty."

But instead of chuckling at the jest, the Queen eyed Mellie thoughtfully. "You really suspect Lachlan Fraser?"

Immediately serious once more, Mellie dropped her

hands and nodded. "The Grants told us he was a traitor, just like his da. The attack came during his audience with ye. And the assassin called him by name when asked who employed him."

Rosa was shaking her head, ticking off points on her fingers. "The Grant warrior might've said whatever he thought ye wished to hear. The timing of the attack could be coincidence. And the assassin might've been calling out to Ross, who was kneeling beside him—we all agreed on that. *De omnibus dubitandum.*"

Charlotte hummed. "So ye don' believe the Fraser is behind the attack, Rosalind?"

Pursing her lips, the youngest Angel tilted her head to stare upward, as she always did when she considered all possible angles of a problem. The others knew her well enough to stay silent, but finally, her shoulders slumped with a sigh.

"Nay," she admitted, pressing the heels of her hands against her eyes in surrender. "He is still our likeliest suspect."

"I want him followed," Elizabeth snapped out. "If he meets with another assassin, or has any other dealings with this Red Hand organization, I want—"

"I'll do it."

Mellie's offer surprised them all, including herself.

She hadn't thought through her words, and when Rosa frowned at her, Mellie couldn't think of a single reason *why* she should be the one to trail the Fraser. But when Charlotte objected, Mellie felt herself bristle.

"Absolutely no'," the pregnant woman said, rifling through the rosters on her desk. "Murtaugh, or his brother—"

"—will stick out like mutton in Lent." Mellie pushed herself to her feet, the embroidery dangling forgotten from one fist. "I *can* do it. He'll no' suspect me."

Charlotte's gaze turned speculative. "He is a good-looking man…is that it?"

No matter what abilities she had, Mellie would never be as smart as Rosa, nor as brave and strong as Court. Long ago, she'd accepted her role in their team and *knew* she was good at it.

She understood people.

Aye, she enjoyed the pleasure found in a man's arms, and aye, she knew how to capitalize on a man's desires. It was a role she understood, and one which had saved their arses more than once.

But there were times she wished the others might see her as more than simply a whore.

Tears pricked at the back of Mellie's eyes, and her other hand curled into a fist. But she had years of practice of not letting anyone see how much their casual assumptions might hurt. So she swallowed down her bitterness and lifted her chin, saying what she knew they all expected.

"Aye. Mayhap I'll find a way to make him confess."

Still, Charlotte shook her head. " 'Tis too dangerous—"

"Let her do it."

Mellie wasn't the only one surprised by the Queen's command—and her support. Charlotte's scowl swung to her friend, but Elizabeth was gazing at Mellie in speculation.

"Melisandre is a strong young woman, and I believe she can handle the Fraser."

Charlotte sucked in a slow breath, then made a sound suspiciously like a *harrumph*. But surprisingly, she didn't make a joke about *handling* the Fraser.

Had Mellie's heart not been pounding against her ribs, her throat burning in bitterness for a situation she was responsible for, she might've made the joke herself.

It was what she did, after all.

"Fine," the pregnant woman finally snapped, then released

a heavy sigh. "But Murtaugh and Tearlach will be yer backup in case ye cannae tail the Fraser." She lifted a stylus, but before she could make a note on her roster, she pointed the implement at Mellie. "But ye'll take care. Swear it, Mellie. If the Fraser is responsible for this assassin, only the Devil himself kens what the man is capable of."

Slowly, not quite believing they had agreed—and not quite sure what had made her volunteer in the first place—Mellie swallowed and nodded. "I swear," she managed to say, around the lump in her throat.

Thrusting herself to her feet, Elizabeth nodded firmly. "Then it's settled. I will send the King a missive with the news myself. Rosalind, you and Charlotte will keep your minds whirling in case there's more suspects."

Rosa jumped to her feet and curtsied prettily. "And I'll keep her seated too, Yer Majesty."

"Good," Elizabeth said with a small smile, glancing at her best friend. "And as soon as that babe decides he is ready, you will call for me *and* the midwives."

"Aye, *Yer Majesty*," Charlotte said with a roll of her eyes and a deep sigh. "Liam will likely be useless, after all."

"They always are," Elizabeth agreed. "And Melisandre?"

Mellie straightened her shoulders, her fingers digging into the silk of her gown to hide their shaking. "Aye, my Queen?"

The older woman held her gaze. "Good luck."

CHAPTER 1

*S*cotland, 1320

*L*aird Lachlan Fraser of Lovat had a headache, but that was no surprise. He *always* had a headache when he was forced to visit Scone.

Was it the gossip? The incessant, meaningless chatter? The perfumes the women and courtiers drenched themselves with?

Or was it merely yesterday's blow to his head?

He wasn't sure, but the pressure had begun building behind his eyes almost the moment they'd arrived three days ago, and yesterday's debacle had only made it worse.

Gillepatric had spent most of the journey to Scone lecturing Lachlan about his duties as Fraser laird, and how important it was to appear at his best in front of the Queen.

As if Lachlan were a mere lad. As if he'd never attended court before!

I met Alice here, did I no'?

Aye, one more reason to hate the place.

Were all the women in the Queen's retinue as cold and heartless as Alice Stewart had been?

Likely not, but that didn't stop Lachlan from disliking them.

Sighing, he pinched at the bridge of his nose, hoping the effort would make the headache go away.

It didn't.

Still, he forced himself to breath deeply as he crossed the courtyard toward the gate, his hand resting loosely on the hilt of his sword. When the guards on duty eyed him with suspicion, he lifted his hand in greeting and attempted a smile.

Though that didn't work either.

The men—both wearing royal badges—fingered their own blades and glared at him, as he slipped, alone, out of the Scone fortress, which housed the royal family and all of their hangers-on.

Honestly, he couldn't blame them.

If Lachlan thought court was bad, then the last day had been four times worse.

He'd spent the hours being glared at by everyone from the servants to his own men. His old friend, Ross, had returned to the Queen's service after Lachlan had released him, but hadn't even bothered to come by Lachlan's assigned chambers to update him.

Mayhap he hadn't been able.

*Y*esterday morning, right in the middle of Lachlan's impassioned vow of fealty to the Queen of Scotland, a man dressed as a servant had thrown down his cups and slammed Lachlan in the side of the head with a tray.

That had only been the beginning of the pandemonium, as the man had then used Lachlan's distraction to pull a blade and leap for the monarch. Having left his blade at the door of the throne room to show his loyalty—and his head ringing from the blow—Lachlan had been damn near useless.

Still, he would've jumped without a thought to put himself between his Queen and the assassin, had Gillepatric not stopped him.

The bearded man's grip on his arm had been enough to swing Lachlan about, and just as he'd opened his mouth to ask his mother's advisor what in *damnation* he thought he was doing, a shout went up from the crowd.

Lachlan had pulled away in time to see the assassin go down with an arrow in his chest, and Ross—along with a strangely dressed woman, carrying a bow—racing for the attacker. The other guards had been trying to clear the throne room, but Lachlan stood firm for the time it took to hear Ross question the dying man.

When asked who'd sent him, the man had said only, "Fraser," as he reached for Ross and left a large bloody handprint on Lachlan's friend's chest.

Cursing, Lachlan had stepped forward then, determined to assure Her Majesty his clan was innocent of these charges, but Gillepatric had tugged on him most insistently.

"Come along, milord," the older man had hissed in his ear. " 'Tis enough excitement for one morn, and ye'll have time to plead yer case when things have calmed down, and the Queen is thinking properly."

The suggestion had been wise, and with a sigh, Lachlan swallowed down his anger and allowed himself to be shooed out of the room.

Mayhap there was a reason Gillepatric had been a Fraser advisor for so long. He'd stood at Lachlan's father's side, then at his elder brother Hamish's side. Now that Lachlan had the role of laird—which he'd *never* aspired to—the older man had been spending more time with Lachlan's mother, who claimed he was a brilliant advisor.

But Lachlan had always preferred his own council, to that of a man so obviously stuck in the past. He was grateful Ross had obtained a group of advisors for him as well, but had chosen to only bring Gillepatric with him, not expecting this meeting to be anything more than routine.

Still, his suggestion to retreat had had some merit, and Lachlan returned to his chambers, fully expecting a summons, which never came. Instead, he'd spent the hours being peered at and muttered about.

Even now, away from the palace and among the commoners of Scone, he couldn't shake the feeling of being watched.

But I'm away from the judging eyes of court, and that's what matters.

He breathed deep, noting how different the scents were out here, away from the perfumes and incense and candles of the palace. The acrid smells coming from the tanner's mixed with the tantalizing whiffs of fresh-baked bread from the baker's a few doors down.

Here in Scone, the buildings were packed closer together than at home, and while there was some delineation of professions and order to the city's design, everywhere Lachlan looked, he saw chaos.

It was certainly *interesting*, wasn't it?

In the central square, merchant apprentices were calling out their wares, while cart drivers yelled at one another over who deserved the right-of-way. Housewives haggled with clerks over the price of fish, and one portly man cursed loudly and shook his fist at an urchin, who was running away with a stolen apple.

Chaos, indeed.

Simone would love this.

The thought caused his lips to twitch upwards, though just slightly

Aye, she would indeed. She would have been standing there beside him, her hand in his, breathlessly scanning the crowds and trying to decide which direction to head to first.

Lachlan's eyes lit on a cart selling woven ribbons. Likely, Simone would've tugged him in that direction as soon as she'd seen it.

Well, he admitted to himself, chuckling slightly, *a pretty ribbon would make a fine gift.*

Mayhap then she'd forgive him for leaving her back home, while he went off "on an adventure," as she'd accused.

Some adventure.

Out here in the square, his headache had lessened, despite the noise. Likely because he had no need to pretend to be someone he wasn't.

Likely because no one suspected him of treason.

He reached the ribbon seller and offered the man a tight greeting as he perused his wares. A long ribbon of deep blue caught Lachlan's eye, reminding him of his loch at sunset. He pulled it down, and when the seller told him the price, reached into the pouch at his waist for the coin.

Their business complete, he folded the ribbon to slip into the pouch, but then froze, *sure* he felt eyes on him.

Slowly he turned, scanning the crowd around him.

He was a warrior, aye, and would fight if necessary. By His Blood, he'd had to do so often enough, even as a lad. Even when his older brother Hamish had been laird, the Frasers had been in more battles and feuds than had been healthy.

But since the Bruce had secured Scottish independence—since Lachlan had become laird—his clan had been focused on rebuilding. On *peace*.

While he'd prefer not to fight at all, he'd still defend himself. If this itchy feeling between his shoulder blades meant an attack was coming, his sword would be ready.

But as he searched, he saw nothing suspicious. No one watched him; no one even stood still in the sea of chaos, which would attract his attention.

Nay, everything seemed normal.

"What ails ye?" the ribbon seller snapped.

Lachlan shook himself. Back home, no one spoke to him that way anymore, and all would refer to him in some way, either as "Laird" or "milord" or even just plain "Fraser."

But he'd never wanted those titles, and it was nice, occasionally, to be snapped at like a normal man. So he shook his head, took a deep breath, and nodded to the seller.

"Naught ails me. Thank ye."

The man nodded gruffly in return. "Yer lady will like it, methinks. Watch yer purse in the crowds, aye?"

Lachlan moved on, considering the man's words.

He'd been to Scone and other cities more than a few times, and knew to keep a watch on his valuables. A man of his size, carrying a sword so openly, likely had little to worry about, but still…

He ducked into the shadows between two buildings—a sort of alleyway, with a stream of refuse sluggishly crawling down the center—and adjusted his belt. He moved his pouch to his left hip, beside his sword, to make it harder for a thief to grab. Then he settled his hand atop his hilt and straightened his shoulders, intent on rejoining the mass of humanity in the square.

And he would've done so, had he not felt a blade between his shoulders.

Damnation.

"Turn around slow," came the growled command behind him.

Lachlan cocked his head. "Nay, I don' think so."

"Ye donae get to *think*, whoreson! Turn around, and let's see that purse ye're being so free with."

One hand on the hilt of his sword, Lachlan placed the other on his opposite hip and stared out at the people rushing by him.

They were close enough to hear him if he called out, but would they help him?

Internally, he shrugged, knowing he wouldn't call out even if he needed to. He'd not put anyone else in danger, if he could help it.

In a curious tone, he asked, "Surely ye ken all I have to do is step forward, out of yer reach? I could kill ye then."

When the blade pressed into his flesh, Lachlan winced. If he bled all over this shirt, Gillepatric would find out, then *Mother* would find out, and he'd never hear the end of it.

"Fine," he sighed, then stepped forward.

But instead of hurrying away, he turned, as the thief wanted, and faced the man.

Or rather…*men*.

There were two: a small skinny one with a ratty beard, and a barrel-chested oaf, who glared as if he didn't oft need to speak.

He raised a brow, silently prodding for the next step in this bizarre dance between them.

The smaller man nodded, pleased. "We could've just slit yer purse strings, ye ken, had ye not moved it." He held out his hand and wiggled his fingers encouragingly. "So just untie it again and hand it over."

Lachlan thought of the blue ribbon in his pouch, and how much Simone would like it.

"Nay," he repeated, "I don' think I will."

The man's pleasant look faded into a scowl. "Then ye can *die*. Hodan?"

The great bull of a man stepped forward with a growl as Lachlan's knuckles tightened around the hilt of his sword. The blade was already half out of the scabbard when a piercing whistle echoed through the alley, and both cutpurses froze.

From the shadows at the other end of the alley, a male figure, anger radiating with every stride, stormed toward them. "Rhys! Hodan! Ye abandon yer posts for *thieving?*"

The smaller man opened his mouth to respond, but the newcomer—a blond man, dressed in simple leather trewes and a green tunic—grabbed him by the scruff and shook him. "I *kenned* I couldnae trust ye two."

"Aww, leave off, milord," the man—Rhys?—whined. "We were following him, as ye asked."

"And ye thought to make a profit while ye're at it?" the newcomer growled. "I told ye, we are done with the Red Hand. If ye follow me still, ye take my orders."

The barrel-chested man was bobbing his head and his shoulders—giving the appearance much like a chicken—as he made apologetic grunts. The blond man, who was obviously their leader, pushed Rhys toward him.

"Get back to yer posts. I want *information*, no' purses."

"Aye, milord," the smaller man whined, as he bobbed his head along with his partner. "We'll watch the gates."

Rhys scowled at Lachlan as he and Hodan squeezed past him on their way out of the alley. Turning his shoulders so he could watch them go, Lachlan slid his sword back home, careful not to release his grip until he knew the danger had truly passed.

When the pair disappeared into the crowd, and he was satisfied they wouldn't attack his back, at least without raising too much suspicion, Lachlan turned back to the stranger in the alley.

"My thanks."

The man met his eyes, and even in the dim light, Lachlan saw *something* flash in them, although he couldn't tell their color.

Alarm, mayhap?

The cutpurses' leader sucked in a breath as his nostrils flared, then turned, giving Lachlan his shoulder, his attention focused on the wall beside him, as if he couldn't stand to look at Lachlan.

"Ye're a Fraser," the man bit out.

That much was obvious from the plaid Lachlan wore.

"Aye, and who is the Red Hand?" It was likely rude to push for answers when the man had just saved his purse and Simone's ribbon, but Lachlan wasn't exactly in a polite frame of mind. "And why are ye watching the palace?"

When the man swallowed, Lachlan could see the muscles flexing in his jaw, and the pause before he spoke seemed to Lachlan to mean he wasn't sure how to answer.

Or was trying to keep his lies straight.

Finally, without looking at him, the blond stranger spoke tightly. "I am looking for…a woman. In the palace."

Lachlan's gaze traveled over the man's simple garb. He was clearly no nobleman, and the woman he was looking for could not be a lady.

"Well, I have come from the palace, as yer men told ye. I might be able to help ye, as ye've helped me."

The man closed his eyes briefly, then let out a slow breath. As he turned, Lachlan saw movement behind him, in the shadows against one of the buildings. *Something* rose from the stack of crates and refuse, but before he could see it clearly, the blond man faced him once more, his shoulders held back and his gaze direct.

It was Lachlan's turn to frown.

God's Blood, but the man seemed…*familiar*, somehow.

"Her name is Courtney," the man said. "I've tracked her thus far, but her trail ends at the palace—"

His words were cut off by the blade which materialized at the blond man's throat.

Behind him, a shape rose up, and a voice—a *female* voice—hissed, "Ye'll *never* get yer filthy claws into her again, ye Red Hand scum!"

The blond stranger had frozen, eyes wide. But between one heartbeat and the next, his shoulders relaxed, his chin dropped, and Lachlan *knew* his plan. Knew it, because it was what Lachlan himself would do in that same situation. Knew it, because his Uncle Andrew had taught him how to fight back with a blade at his throat, and this man was prepared to do the same: lower his shoulder, kick back, and duck to the side, while grabbing and *yanking* the assailant.

And he would've succeeded, but Lachlan knew he couldn't allow it. He couldn't allow any man to harm a woman.

So before the blond stranger could step into his attack, Lachlan darted forward, his hand taking hold of the front of the man's tunic, before slamming his fist into the other man's jaw.

Lachlan had tried to direct the force away from the woman, but the blond stranger's head snapped back and knocked against her cheekbone, causing her to flinch away. Luckily, she had the presence of mind to pull the blade—a long, wicked looking dagger—away from the man's throat, rather than spilling more blood on the filthy cobblestones.

To Lachlan's surprise, she only released a hiss of pain from the blow. The blond stranger was knocked cold before he could utter a sound.

The entire encounter took less than a few seconds, and was almost completely silent.

Allowing the dead weight of the man to slip from his hand and slump senseless on the ground, Lachlan stepped toward his unlikely savior. The woman, who was currently staring, horrified, at the body on the ground, also looked familiar.

What in damnation was wrong with him, that he kept seeing familiar faces everywhere he turned today?

As he stepped forward, she stumbled back, the blade gripped tightly in her hand, and and her wide eyes locked onto him. Recognition finally slammed into him.

She'd been there, just yesterday, in the throne room!

She appeared to be some sort of servant, surely, dressed as she'd been in a too-tight kirtle and drab gown. Today, she wore dark gray, which had allowed her to blend into the shadows, but her dress was just as equally humble.

Lachlan stretched out a hand to her, patting the air in a soothing gesture. "Shh," he murmured. " 'Tis aright. He cannae hurt ye now."

"*Hurt* me?" The woman shook her head. "He's *unconscious*! Do ye have any idea how much *force* it takes to knock a man out cold like that? He'll likely have brain damage or— God above, I'm rambling."

'Tis likely hysteria.

Lachlan tried a charming grin. "And do ye care? If he's damaged?"

The woman blew out a breath, which caused her breasts to do all sorts of interesting things, and shook her head. " 'Twould've been nice to question him about the Red Hand, but ye're safe, and that's what matters."

"*I'm* safe?" Lachlan asked incredulously.

"Aye, and ye're welcome for saving ye."

Was it possible the woman *wasn't* having hysterics?

God Above knew, between Simone's tantrums and Mother's antics, he was used to womanly theatrics. But this particular woman didn't seem at all concerned about the violence she'd just witnessed...and had a part in.

On the contrary, as he watched, she bent over and yanked up her skirts, revealing a pair of boots and smooth stockings —the silk at odds with the course wool of her gown—and a leather sheath. With a smooth, practiced motion, she tucked the long dagger back into the leather, fluffed her skirts back over it, then straightened so quickly, Lachlan wondered if he'd imagined it all.

But nay, there she stood, without a dagger, her hands folded in front of her and smiling up at him in a sort of patronizing way.

"Aye," she said slowly, as if he were hard of understanding. "Ye are safe. Now, be about yer business." She unclasped her hands long enough to make a little shooing motion. "Forget ye saw me."

Forget...?

Lachlan snorted, his lips curving upward.

Forget this angel in front of him?

If anything, he'd likely store this vision in his memory and pull it out when he was alone with only his hand for company. Now that he could see her clearly, and the threat of danger was past, he felt himself stir at the sight. She was exactly the sort of woman he'd always fancied, and as far from Alice's slender form as possible.

This woman, his *savior*, had thick curls—the color of spun gold, with ribbons of a light reddish color shimmering throughout—pulled back in a braid, which was fighting a losing battle against the curled tendrils loosely flowing around her forehead and ears.

Her skin appeared to have been kissed by the sun, her luminescent eyes, of a startling sapphire blue, were perfectly placed above a cute, pert nose and deliciously luscious full lips.

And her body!

Lachlan took a moment to allow his gaze to drift lower, appreciating what he saw. She was curvy in all the right places, the sort of hips a man might *appreciate* for hours. And her breasts—

She cleared her throat. "My eyes are up here."

Chagrined, but not quite knowing why, his gaze snapped up to hers again, only to realize she was…*blushing?*

God's Blood, had he made her uncomfortable?

"I'm sorry, lass. What were ye saying?"

She frowned. "I was *telling* ye to move along, to forget this happened. Go back to the palace where ye belong, Fraser."

She knew him?

"I don' belong in that palace any more than—than—" He shook his head, unable to come up with an analogy. "I donae belong there, and I'll be leaving as soon as possible."

One golden brow rose. "Ye're leaving?"

"Aye." Though he couldn't understand why he was explaining himself to a serving wench, he continued, "I've done what I needed to do here in Scone."

Before yesterday's excitement, he'd finished his oath of loyalty to the crown, and thought the Queen had been satisfied. Now, however, he just needed to hear she thought him blameless for the fiasco yesterday, and he could return home in peace.

"I'm only waiting on the Queen's summons once more, to be finished."

"I see."

Although it was dark here in the alley, he saw her lips thin and her expression draw in, as if she disapproved. She stepped back, out of his reach, and when she spoke next, her tone had become icy.

"Go on then. Finish what ye started, if ye think ye can."

With those baffling words, she turned and was soon

embraced back into the shadows where she'd come from. He watched until she disappeared entirely, his arms folded thoughtfully across his chest and his weight on one hip, as she slipped toward the other end of the alley, moving from shadow to shadow, her steps careful and measured, as if she were used to moving about in secret.

A bizarre skill for a serving wench.

He was tempted to go after her, to track her back to her lair, to corner her, to demand answers. He wanted to press her against a wall, to feel those heavy breasts heaving against his chest as he used his lips to tease answers from her.

Under his kilt, his cock stirred at the thought, and he growled in irritation. Aye, she was a fine-looking woman, but he had only to remember the sight of her with that dagger in her hand and the irritation he'd heard in her voice when she caught him staring at her body, to know she wouldn't give up answers easily.

Not the way he'd like, at least.

She'd appeared like some sort of protecting angel, intent on *saving* him, which was both galling and intriguing.

If she served in the palace, mayhap he'd find a reason to stay in Scone longer?

As if to chastise him, his headache chose that moment to return with a vengeance, a heavy pounding behind his eyes which made him wince.

Nay. Nay, there were bold, golden-haired wenches at home. Mayhap none as curvy as her, but he'd simply close his eyes and remember her.

Besides, home meant no more headaches. Home meant peaceful evenings by his loch and moments spent curled up with Simone, and hunting in his woods.

He didn't belong here, but she did.

With a sigh, he shook his head, wishing the headache

away. It hadn't bothered him during the time he'd been in danger, but now it was back with a vengeance.

"God's Blood," he muttered, and turned away from the alley and the unconscious man he couldn't recall how he knew. "This isnae for me."

Home was calling.

CHAPTER 2

"Tell me everything."

Rosa pulled Mellie into Charlotte's private study and pushed the door shut behind them. At her command, Charlotte looked up from her papers and frowned. The pregnant woman glanced between her two remaining Angels—Rosa, whose lips were pursed determinedly, and Mellie, who looked completely exhausted—and nodded.

"Aye, tell her everything. But do it from a chair, with a glass of wine."

Her mentor's humor never failed to lighten Mellie's heart, but today she couldn't manage much more than a weak smile. She'd been trailing Lachlan Fraser since early that morning, and after the disastrous encounter in the alleyway, had been more than happy to pass the duty off to one of the Queen's guards for a bit.

She gratefully took the vessel of wine Rosa passed her. "That man has the longest legs in the history of legs."

Charlotte snorted. "Couldn't keep up with him?"

"Oh, I could." Mellie sipped from the cup as she reached

down to rub her knees with her empty hand. "But I'm no' built for running after a man."

"Aye?" her mentor asked distractedly. "What *are* ye built for?"

"Love."

Love.

Sainte Vierge, but that sounded pitiful.

When Rosa shot a look Mellie's way, which told her her wistfulness had been a bit too obvious, she hastened to add a lewd wink. She wanted her teammate to believe she'd meant *physical* love, and nothing more.

Six years ago, she'd had those secret yearnings crushed, when she'd learned all she was *really* good for.

She'd learned she *was* built for love, but only the kind a man wanted temporarily. Mayhap not the kind she'd dreamed of, the kind she'd wanted when she was younger…but she'd learned to use her *build* to her advantage.

And hide the part of her which still ached for a child of her own and the eternal love of a special man.

When Charlotte tossed down her stylus and stretched with a grimace, Mellie had to look away to hide her jealousy. There'd been a point in her life when *she* had been lucky enough to experience the aches pregnancy brought, as well as the thrill of feeling her unborn child move.

Sainte Vierge!

What was wrong with her?

Why was she being so…maudlin?

"Aye, well"—Charlotte exhaled deeply—"as long as *men* are built for love as well, aye?"

Knowing what was expected of her, Mellie pushed down her thoughts and chuckled throatily, lifting her cup to her lips.

But Rosa was still frowning. "What does a man's build

have to do with— Oh. Ye're talking about his penis, are ye no'?"

This time, Charlotte was the one to burst out in surprised laughter.

Mellie saluted her young friend with her cup. " 'Tis the only part that matters!"

Rosalind was brilliant, aye, but more than willing to bow to Mellie—and even Court's—knowledge of the world. When it came to men, she was hopeless and put up with everyone's teasing good-naturedly.

Calming herself at last, Charlotte planted her elbows on the desk. "Well? Report."

Mellie took a deep breath, then began, pleased to be dealing with what mattered once more. She closed her eyes and told the pair everything the Fraser laird had done that day, from the moment he'd exited his chambers. Most of it was likely to be irrelevant, but if anyone could find something of importance, it'd be Rosa.

It wasn't until she spoke of her excursion into Scone, that her voice faltered. She opened her eyes to see Rosa perched on the edge of the desk, staring out the window, while Charlotte nodded encouragingly.

"Who was he meeting?"

Mellie shrugged. "He seemed to be just…shopping. He bought a ribbon from a seller."

"A ribbon?" Charlotte's brows went up. "For a lady love?"

"Or to defer suspicion," Rosa murmured, not looking at them, as her mind whirled. "Continue please."

Apparently, nothing Fraser had done so far was enough to cause Rosa to ask for clarification, so Mellie told about the man's encounter with the two cutpurses, and how she'd snuck around the back of the alley to help him.

"By the time I arrived, they were gone, but another was in their place. He was speaking to Fraser, and they appeared…

equals?" She shook her head, unable to explain the sensation that the two were similar. "I thought mayhap this was a compatriot I'd never seen, but as I approached, the man was clearly uncomfortable in Fraser's presence. He was asking about Courtney."

As Charlotte gasped, Rosa turned, her blue eyes piercing Mellie with their intensity. "Tell me everything."

Mellie did, trying her best to recount every nuance of the stranger's presence, his conversation with Fraser, her own attack, and both men's reaction. She told them of Fraser's words and actions after the brief skirmish, including the appreciative gleam in his gray eyes when he'd raked her body with his gaze.

But she left out the way his piercing regard had made her *feel*.

She was no simpering virgin, new to desire. Fraser was a fine-looking man, aye, and that was all there was to it.

"The man he was speaking to"—Rosa shook her head—"was no' just a member of the Red Hand, but a man who obviously knows Court. When she returns…"

Charlotte nodded. "Aye, she'll have much to report herself, I'll wager. But there's naught we can do about the stranger. Fraser is our focus."

"He said he had done what he needed to do here in Scone, and once he saw the Queen once more, he'd be finished."

Rosa, bless her, cursed in Latin, as was her wont.

Charlotte wasn't nearly so polite.

"By St. Ninian's left foot!" she growled, reaching for her roster. "I'll have Liam treble the Queen's guard!"

With shaking fingers, Mellie placed the cup on the desk.

Was she really so tired?

Or was her reaction based on fear?

"The Queen is planning on seeing him?"

"Aye," Charlotte snapped, as she made notes. "She told me

herself she planned on calling another audience, since their first one was so rudely interrupted. I donae ken what she'll say to the man, but we can ensure she's well-guarded."

Rosa glanced at Mellie. "We'll be at her side."

Mellie's agreement was slower than it should have been.

"Mellie?" Rosa prompted.

" 'Tis nothing."

'Tis everything.

To her surprise, Mellie didn't *want* to be any nearer to Fraser than she had to be. The way he'd looked at her...

She swallowed. She was used to those looks, certainly, but the way her body had *reacted* to him? *That* was the true surprise.

Charlotte looked up, meeting Mellie's eyes. "Can ye do it, Mel? Do ye want me to turn yer assignment over to another?"

Who?

Rosa?

Mellie met her friend's eyes before the younger woman flushed and looked away.

Nay, someone as innocent as Rosa couldn't be asked to deal with Fraser. A man who looked at Mellie the way he had was clearly being led through life by his cock, and Mellie...?

Well, Mellie knew how to use that to her advantage. Rosa did not.

"Nay," she finally managed, shaking her head and pretending not to see Rosa's small relieved sigh. "I'll do it."

"Good. Because the Queen—"

"I owe Elizabeth everything," Mellie snapped. "She gave me a place when my own family wouldnae look at me. I'll do whatever I need to do to protect her."

The words sat like a gauntlet between them, and part of Mellie prayed Charlotte wouldn't pick it up.

But for all that Charlotte was a good friend, she was the

Queen's spy-mistress first, and knew her duty was to the royal family *and* to Scotland, and so she nodded. "Then go rest. I'm sure Her Majesty's summons will come ere long."

~

Thank the saints the Queen's summons had finally come!

Lachlan wasn't sure how much longer he could stand to be stuck there in the palace. Since returning to his chambers yesterday—after that strange encounter in Scone—he'd rarely left since. He'd even taken his meals alone in his rooms, hoping it would diminish the suspicion clearly still directed his way.

It hadn't.

As he and Gillepatric, and a few of the loyal Fraser warriors he'd brought along with him, strode through the palace halls to meet with the Queen, he felt eyes on him and could easily hear the whispers from all he passed.

I'll be home soon.

Then all of this—the headache, the suspicions, the memories of that delicious serving wench—would be far behind him.

Well, mayhap not.

Despite the seriousness of the situation, one corner of Lachlan's mouth pulled up as he remembered those wide delectable lips of hers. He'd taken himself in hand last night, imagining those lips on his body, and he'd even briefly considered attempting to track her down. She was here in the palace *somewhere*, and he wanted to know what in damnation she'd been thinking yesterday in that alley.

He wanted to know what kind of woman thought *he* needed protection. He wanted to ask her what the Red Hand was all about, and what it had to do with the assassin.

But he was honest enough to admit, if he ever found her, *talking* would be the last thing on his mind.

Under his kilt—freshly brushed, with perfect pleats for his audience with the Queen—his cock stirred. He swallowed, forcing himself to breathe deeply and focus on the coming meeting, knowing he couldn't afford to be distracted.

Nay, this audience was all-important.

It was well-known that his father, Michael Fraser, had not supported the Bruce's claim to the throne of Scotland. Lachlan's brother, Hamish, who was the next laird, might've had his own perverse hobbies, but at least he was not an outright traitor as their father had been.

It was Lachlan's hope this visit to Scone would assure the Crown he was nothing like his father. He supported King Robert wholeheartedly and would do anything the man asked to ensure a free and peaceful Scotland.

Unfortunately, some damn inopportune timing on the part of the assassin meant the Frasers were once again under royal suspicion.

When they reached the doors to the throne room, the guards demanded his weapons. Although it irked him to lose his sword, he was quick to turn it and his dagger over to show the Crown it had nothing to fear from him or his men.

Aye, this meeting might be the one which determined the fate of all the Frasers, and he'd not jeopardize his clan's peaceful future.

Taking a deep breath, he stepped into the throne room, the reassurance of his advisor's presence beside him, and crossed to where the Queen sat on a dais once more. He placed his fist against his heart and bowed low, hoping Elizabeth would take it for the show of respect it was.

"Rise, Lachlan Fraser," came her imperious command.

As he lifted his head, he found himself glancing around the room hopefully. Was he looking for Ross, despite knowing his friend wasn't here? Ross had been raised with Lachlan, training together. After Bannockburn, his friend had returned to Scone with the Bruce to protect his lady wife. It was only two years ago, when Lachlan had become laird, that he'd asked Ross to return home to help him with the transition. But now that he was settled as the Fraser, he'd happily given Ross leave to return to his position at court, guarding the Queen.

Not that there weren't enough guards around the Queen. He recognized any number of tartans before he turned his attention back where it belonged.

"Thank ye for seeing me again, Yer Majesty. I ken our last audience was interrupted, and ye cannae ken how pleased I am that ye werenae harmed."

Elizabeth's lips pursed as she stared down at him. Finally, she nodded regally. "You must know, Lord Fraser, that many wonder if you were behind the attack."

Lachlan's brows rose. Not because he was surprised by the accusation, but because he hadn't expected her to state it so baldly. As someone who spoke plainly, and who hated the polite lies and distortions of court, it was a refreshing turn of events.

"They are wrong, Yer Majesty," he stated clearly. "I am a loyal Highlander and would do naught to harm my King or his family."

"It has not always been so, I believe?" The Queen's words were thoughtful, as if she wondered what his reaction might be. "Your father, for instance, did not support my husband's campaign for the throne."

"Aye," he quickly agreed. It was the truth after all. "My father was a traitor to the Scottish cause. I'm here now to assure ye 'tisnae the case for the present Fraser of Lovat."

The Queen hummed low in her throat, her dark eyes searching Lachlan's, as if looking for sincerity. He straightened his shoulders, rested his hands on his hips, and did his best to show her he had nothing to hide.

"Yer Majesty," he said in a low voice, "all I want is peace for my people."

"I suspect that is the case for all leaders, Lord Fraser," she replied noncommittally.

Damnation.

Lachlan wasn't sure this was going well.

Not for the first time, he reflected on the light of intelligence in the Queen's eyes.

This was no pampered court lady, used to getting her way. Queen Elizabeth had spent eight long years as a prisoner of the English, and since her return five years ago, had borne two royal princesses, and managed the court in Robert's absence.

She was wily, and so very unlike the other ladies he knew.

He'd do well to remember that.

Unconsciously, his eyes drifted to her left where a cluster of her ladies sat on a bench. Two of them were whispering behind their hands to one another, while another—a slender dark-skinned beauty with a sharp gaze—watched him intently. He jerked his eyes away from her, not sure he wanted to give another female the chance to try to second-guess him, and noticed the golden-haired woman standing behind the bench.

He sucked in a breath.

It was *her*.

His brows pulled in tightly before he could stop himself.

What in the name of all the saints of Heaven was *she* doing here in the throne room, standing beside the Queen, and dressed like a princess?

The curvy beauty from yesterday met his eyes defiantly, her own snapping with some sort of challenge. The red silk gown she wore did everything right to accentuate her hips and breasts, and her curls hung loose down her back.

Though it wasn't an accepted court style, but the sight made Lachlan's pulse pound, and his cock twitch.

God Almighty, but she was a vision. One he very much wanted to touch, to taste!

What was she doing in the throne room?

Was she *not* a serving wench as he'd thought?

Was it possible she was…a *lady*?

He blanched at the thought, not just because of the things he'd been fantasizing about doing to her, but what it meant about her as a whole.

Alice had been a lady, and he'd met her here, in this very throne room, long before—

"Lord Fraser!"

The Queen's barked command dragged his attention guiltily away from the golden-haired enigma.

"Aye, Yer Majesty?" he managed.

"You claim you are loyal to the Crown?" She stood, and when she did, her ladies stood as well. "You will prove this."

Lachlan placed his fist over his heart. "Anything, Yer Majesty."

He meant his words. He *was* loyal to the Bruce and welcomed the chance to prove it.

The Queen nodded. "Ye will marry."

His brows flew up once more, as his vision immediately began to tunnel at the Queen's command.

"Marry?" He shook his head. "Yer Majesty, Simone—" How to explain he neither needed, nor wanted, a wife? "She is all I…"

He was a making a mess of this, and he knew it. Taking a deep breath, he lifted his chin and stated firmly, "I need no wife, my Queen."

"Mayhap." Elizabeth stared down at him for a long

moment. "But you will take one. One of *my* choosing. You are not betrothed, not married. You are free to make an alliance, and I will make one for you. Lady Melisandre Lamond!" she barked suddenly, holding Lachlan's gaze. "Step forward!"

Alarmed, his eyes flew to the woman he'd been fantasizing about, who was now stepping around the bench to reach the Queen's side. Her expression was a careful mask, revealing nothing.

Lady...?

The woman from the alley now had a name.

Melisandre.

But more than that, she had a rank, and she was clearly an expert at the sort of cold calculation he'd witnessed before.

A churning, disgusting feeling filled his gut, clawing its way up his throat to choke him.

Shame.

He was ashamed of the immediate attraction he felt to someone like her.

He'd imagined her warm and willing in his bed. He'd imagined her smiling, those lips pulled wide in laughter.

But now, she was staring down at him, cold and aloof. So different from what he'd thought.

She was just like Alice, was she not?

She was the epitome of everything he'd come to hate.

The Queen spoke again, but Lachlan couldn't tear his gaze away from the deceitful beauty at her side.

"You will prove you are loyal, Lord Fraser, by returning to your home with one of my ladies."

A muscle jumped in the lady's jaw. He lifted his gaze to her—*Melisandre's*—eyes, and saw something he hadn't expected to see: a mixture of irritation and surprise.

Had she not known the Queen would make this demand of her?

Did she not *want* to marry him?

A brief hope jumped in his chest, before she turned to glare at the Queen.

Elizabeth lifted one regal brow as she met her lady's eyes. "Your vow, Lady Melisandre?"

And with just those words, the lady's shoulders slumped, as if the fight had gone out of her.

"Aye," she whispered, "I remember."

Nodding, the Queen turned back to Lachlan. "You will sign the betrothal papers before you leave. As of now, consider yourself bound to this woman. You will prove you are no traitor."

Is that what it would take? Marriage to a cold, deceptive bitch?

Well, he'd tried it before, and if it would ensure his clan's future, he supposed he could do it again.

"Aye, Yer Majesty," he ground out, between clenched teeth. "For the Frasers, and for Scotland, I'll do as ye command."

Without acknowledging his vow, the Queen turned once more to her lady. "Well, Mellie?"

The golden-haired beauty lifted her eyes once more. "Elizabeth, I—" She stopped and shook her head, as if remembering her place. "Aye, Yer Majesty."

But it seemed the Queen wasn't entirely heartless. She leaned slightly toward the younger woman, dropping her voice low enough, Lachlan wasn't sure he was supposed to overhear her words.

"Take all the time you need, Mellie. We're counting on you."

To his surprise, his unwanted betrothed turned to meet his eyes then. She curled the fingers of her right hand into a fist, and the mask she wore so well dropped back into place as she studied him.

Then she lifted her chin, pulled her shoulders back, and slid her hands down the sides of her gown, accentuating her breasts, while those wide, sensual lips pulled up in a knowing smile.

"I'll no' let ye down, Yer Majesty. I'll marry the Fraser."

CHAPTER 3

A coach?

She was going to have to ride in a coach?

Mellie sighed, hiding her disappointment. The coach in the yard carried the royal insignia, and most of the Queen's ladies-in-waiting would be grateful for such comfort and luxury on their journey to their new home.

But most of the Queen's ladies-in-waiting weren't Angels.

Mellie had spent five years at court, being partnered on missions with her best friends, Rosa and Courtney. She'd slept in fields, in caves, in stables, and even in the rain. She'd spent days wearing the same clothes, hunched in the saddle, following her quarry. She'd known true deprivation and hardship in order to complete her mission for the Queen.

Riding in a fine coach couldn't possibly be as difficult as all that.

"*In proelia iterum,*" Rosa whispered behind her.

Mellie was grateful to sink into her friend's open arms, taking comfort in the younger woman's hug.

"The Queen is sending a message by giving ye one of her coaches for the journey."

Mellie sighed against Rosa's hair. "I ken it. She's reminding me I'm to be a *lady* on this trip, no' an Angel."

It was important the Fraser believe she was nothing more than one of the Queen's ladies.

"Aye," Rosa agreed, her voice low enough, no others could possibly overhear their conversation. "But ye will no' be alone. Brigit will post yer letters, and I will keep ye updated on the investigation here in Scone as we discover more information. If yer *betrothed* truly is behind this attempt on the Queen's life, we must ken it. We *must* ken what else he has planned."

Forcing herself to straighten, Mellie swallowed past the lump in her throat. "I ken, don' worry. I'll do my duty."

Rosa glanced around quickly, taking in the bustle in the yard as servants loaded the last of Mellie's trunks into the wagon, which would accompany her to her "new life." She'd had to send most of her clothing along, to make the transition seem believable. They wanted nothing to convince Fraser she wasn't exactly what she seemed; a spoiled and pampered noblewoman traveling to her future home.

But Mellie had left most of her possessions here at the palace, because when she left Lovat, she would need to travel light. Unlike her journey today.

"Mellie..." Her friend lowered her head so no one could read her lips, but kept her eyes locked on Mellie's. "*Only* yer duty, aye?"

Mellie frowned in confusion, and Rosa sighed.

"I ken what ye think of yerself, my dear friend. What ye're being sent to do, ye think there's only one way to do it."

It was clear what Rosa meant, and Mellie forced a discreet bawdy chuckle she didn't feel. "The best way to learn a man's secrets is in his bed."

"Nay," Rosa whispered sharply, then shook her head. She gripped Mellie's shoulders. "Look at me."

When Mellie's brows rose in surprise, Rosa gave her a little shake.

"The best way to learn a man's secrets is to gain his trust, and his heart, Mellie. Ye can do that in other ways than what ye're considering." Her blue eyes were strangely out of focus. "Ye are worth more than that."

"My duty—"

Rosa shook her again. "Do yer duty. But *only* yer duty. And come back to me in one piece, Mellie."

Her friend was worried for her?

The thought caused the lump in Mellie's throat to expand, wondering if this would be her most dangerous mission yet.

It would be her first without her teammates nearby, and Mellie wasn't certain she could succeed without Rosa's mind and Court's bow there to back her up.

"Good luck, Mellie," Rosa whispered. Mellie, unable to find her voice, managed a stiff nod as her friend pulled her in for another hug.

When she climbed into the coach with Brigit—one of the Queen's maids who'd been assigned to Mellie, and who would accompany her as a confidante—Mellie forced her chin up and her shoulders back.

She *would* succeed.

She *would* find the evidence they needed against Fraser.

She wouldn't fail the Queen.

But her resolve weakened when Fraser himself pulled his mare to a stop beside the coach, looking over the thing with what appeared to be disgust. She wanted to defend the choice, to pretend it was what she wanted, to appear a pampered lady.

But the words stuck in her throat, because honestly, she agreed the carriage was too big, too cumbersome, and too slow.

She instead met his pale gaze and gave him a look, which dared him to speak his thoughts aloud.

He didn't. With a clipped nod, he whirled away from her, directing his horse to the cluster of his men who would ride with them.

"Oooh, milady," Brigit giggled beside her. "Yer so lucky to have such a man who desires ye. Anyone can see it, the way he looks at ye."

Desire?

Nay.

Disgust, mayhap.

Lachlan Fraser had looked at her with desire that day in the alleyway in Scone, when he'd thought her someone she wasn't. But now he looked at her as if she were scum...and *still* thought her someone she wasn't.

Unbidden, a thought rose from a place deep within her heart: *What would he think if he saw me as I truly am?*

Nay. Nay, she wouldn't allow that.

Couldn't allow that.

She was an Angel, and he was her assignment.

She would not fail.

◈

Three days. Three long, godforsaken days.

He and his men could've left Scone and been back at An Torr in half this time, but because of that blasted coach and wagon his *betrothed* required to drag her ungodly amount of fripperies, they were taking forever to return home.

The stops at the inns were bad enough—where Melisandre and her lady's maid sequestered themselves in their room without speaking to anyone—but the travel in between was tortuously slow.

At this rate, it will take a full sennight to reach Simone.

But on the fourth day of travel, Lachlan finally felt some of the tension in his chest ease when he recognized the land. He was close to his loch now, and by all the saints, he would take the time to enjoy it.

So he directed the party to detour toward the cliffs, where he knew the view would be best. Without stopping to see if the others would follow, he urged his horse up the path, eager for a glimpse of home.

When he cantered over the rise, Loch Ness spread out before him, and he threw himself out of the saddle and strode toward the sight.

God's Blood, but he'd missed this!

He stood, legs braced against the tug of the breeze, and inhaled deeply, feeling the band around his chest loosen.

Aye, it was possible the Queen and her court suspected him guilty of treason.

Aye, he'd been saddled with an unwanted, pampered noblewoman as a wife.

Aye, his life was about to get so much worse.

But here, breathing in the scents of Loch Ness, feeling the afternoon sun beating on his shoulders, he was free. He was at peace.

He was almost home.

The saints alone know how long he stood there, soaking up the peace. But when he turned to leave, he was surprised to see his future wife standing some distance away, her hands on her hips.

It was the stance of a woman who was comfortable with her body. One who knew how much power she wielded. One who could make a man do her bidding with just a look.

But she wasn't looking at him, nay. She was looking at his loch.

And Lachlan could swear she was smiling.

Was it possible she appreciated the view as much as he did?

God's Blood, when she smiled like that, she became the wench in the alleyway.

Just who *was* this woman he was to marry?

It took a few moments to pick his way along the rocks to her side, his horse trailing behind. When he reached her, she was wearing the same careful indifferent mask he'd seen in the throne room, and again he wondered at her true self.

Was she truly the cold noblewoman she portrayed herself to be?

Or the lusty wench of his dreams?

He cleared his throat. " 'Tis lovely, is it no'?"

When she turned to face him, her hands now folded demurely before her, her brows were drawn in. "Why are ye suddenly being kind to me?"

He was taken aback. "What do ye mean?"

"Ye've avoided me for days, and now ye want to make polite conversation?"

Crossing his arms in front of his chest, he frowned at her. "Ye're the one avoiding *me*, milady. Ye retire to yer room each night, instead of joining us for meals in the common room. No' only did ye miss the chance to get to ken me, ye've been quite rude."

"Rude?" She lifted one perfect brow. "Never mind, I retract my claim of yer sudden kindness."

The quip was so unexpected, Lachlan couldn't hide his snort of surprise. "When ye say things like that, ye remind me of the wench I met in that alleyway."

A flicker not unlike fear flashed through her eyes, before turning back to the loch. "I donae ken what ye're speaking of."

His eyes widened.

She was going to pretend the fight in the alleyway never happened?

She'd held a knife to a man's throat to *save* Lachlan, which had never happened before.

And now she would claim not to know what he meant?

Reaching out, he touched her elbow. "Do ye still carry the dagger strapped to yer leg?"

Would he have the chance to find out?

She jerked away, but didn't look at him. "Donae touch me!"

Hmm.

"Look, milady...*Melisandre*"—Lachlan sighed and turned away, scrubbing his hand across his face. At least the headache had left him—"neither of us wanted this betrothal, I ken it. But mayhap 'tis time to make peace with the person the Crown said we must marry?"

It was the closest he would come to asking for a peace with her.

She wrapped one arm around her middle, her back to him, as she stared out over the loch. Her shoulders were straight, but he watched her lift one hand, and wondered if she was chewing on her fingernail. It might've been erotic, but all he could think was that the gesture made her appear vulnerable.

She took a breath and dropped her hand, then lifted her chin. Without looking at him, she asked, "Who is Simone?"

Saints above, but she was an enigma, with the way her brain worked. "What?"

When she turned, her expression was haughty. "When the Queen told ye of yer duty, ye mentioned *Simone* in yer protest. Who is she?"

Lachlan's hand dropped to the pouch on his belt, where he still carried the lovely blue ribbon he'd purchased for his favorite lass.

One of Melisandre's brows rose in haughty challenge. "I'll no' allow ye to keep another woman, Fraser. Ye'll have to cast off yer leman."

Favorite lass?

Nay, Simone was his *only* lass.

Seeing this woman—this *lady*—curl her lip as she made her demands was like taking a dunk in the cold loch. She was obviously the same as nearly all the other women he'd ever known: spiteful and cold and jealous. He may be forced to marry her, but he'd not allow another woman like Alice into his heart.

His hand closed into a fist, and he growled low in his throat. Without a word, he turned and stalked away, leaving the haughty bitch to stare out over the loch.

~

Another day passed and it took everything in him not to ride ahead to reach An Torr as quickly as he could. He knew his precious Simone was close, and he would soon feel her arms around him in only a matter of hours.

But duty and responsibility stayed his impetuousness.

If he arrived at An Torr without her, only to then introduce her as his intended wife when she finally arrived on her own, his people would see his rudeness as a lack of respect. If *he* didn't respect her, they wouldn't either, and their future lives together as husband and wife would be miserable.

Their people—their *peace*—would suffer for it.

So nay, he didn't ride ahead and leave her, even with the guards. He moderated his pace, gritted his teeth, and rode as far from that damned coach as he could, though still remaining within sight.

Unfortunately, that meant riding beside Gillepatric, who had already spent the last several hours lecturing on how to improve the Frasers' lives, and every single suggestion sounded as if something Lachlan's father would say.

Even though he held his tongue, answering only when Gillepatric asked an outright question he couldn't avoid, the man just wouldn't take the hint and leave Lachlan to his own misery.

Saints above, his headache was returning!

A spiteful wife, an advisor stuck in the past, and a sennight in the saddle. He was ready to be home.

And then, finally—*finally*—he was.

He couldn't help the way he nudged his horse into a trot as An Torr came into sight. The great stone walls would never rival Castle Urquhart, across the loch, but this was *home.*

An Torr's stone tower rose over the inner bailey, with the crenelated walk providing unrivaled views of the loch and surrounding areas, and to the west, a cliff with a sheer drop to the water below could be found.

He hoped his men would ensure his *betrothed* arrived safely, and his people would forgive him if he arrived ten minutes before her, in his eagerness to see—

"Simone! *Simone!*" he called out, as soon as he reached the courtyard.

Swinging off his horse, he was glad to hand the reins off to the lad who came running, and quickly exchanged greetings with the men who flocked to welcome him home.

He shook hands and slapped backs, enthusiastic and sincere in his greetings, but longing and aching to be united with only one person at the moment.

His headache had dissipated as soon as he'd seen An Torr, and now he was home, he became filled with a perfect sort of certainty.

This is where he belonged, and he could make his future a

good one, even if he had to be yoked to a woman not of his choosing.

For the sake of his people, he *would* find a way to make peace.

"Milord, ye're safe!" the seneschal called from atop the keep's steps. "We expected ye days ago!"

"Aye, Martin!" Lachlan chuckled as he made his way through the throngs. "I was…delayed."

As if on cue, the royal coach rolled through the gate, and the crowd quieted to watch. Looking up at the old steward, Lachlan jerked his head in that direction.

"And there's the reason now. I'll explain later. Where's Simone?"

Martin's weathered face split into a grin. "She couldnae miss the commotion, milord. I'm sure she's—"

"Da! *Da!*" a little voice screamed then, echoing through the keep. "Da's home!"

Lachlan's face split into a smile wide enough to hurt his cheeks as he opened his arms.

From the wide double doors atop the steps, a wee hellion —all tangles and freckles and knobby limbs—burst out of the keep.

"Da!" she screamed again, throwing herself off the steps and into his arms.

He snatched her out of mid-air, laughing aloud with her, as he spun her in a circle. Despite her skirts, she wrapped her legs around his middle and, linking her arms behind his neck, squealed with glee as he turned them.

Lachlan encircled his precious daughter within his arms, and burrowed his nose in her hair.

"Simone," he whispered, when he finally came to a stop.

"I missed ye, Da," she mumbled, her mouth pressed against his shoulder.

He couldn't seem to stop smiling. "I missed ye too, wee hellion. I brought ye something."

With a gasp, she straightened, still holding tight to him, but piercing him with sharp gray eyes. "Is it a baby sister?"

He jerked back, surprised. "What? Nay!"

"A mother then? Ye brought me a mother?"

His mouth dropped open.

Where in damnation had she gotten these ideas?

A ribbon—no matter how lovely—would pale in comparison, if she wanted a gift as grand as a *mother*.

But…he *had* brought home a wife, had he not?

His arms tightened around his precious lass.

Would his betrothed accept Simone?

It was unlikely a lady would accept another's bastard, but he could not—*would* not—have a future without his daughter.

"Aye, lass," he croaked. "Mayhap."

It was then he noticed the silence, and turned, his daughter still in his arms.

She was standing there, the fingers of one hand covering her lips, and her blue eyes wide, staring at him and his daughter.

Lachlan knew shock when he saw it, but he wasn't sure if her ailment was caused by joy, confusion, or horror.

Without loosening his hold on his daughter, he bowed slightly to her, which caused Simone to shriek with laughter and tighten her grip.

"Milady," he managed.

Melisandre's expression didn't change, but now her eyes were locked only on Simone.

"Who is—" She cleared her throat and tried again, dropping her hand into her other, so both were gripped in front of her chest in an almost hopeful pose. "Who is this?"

Lachlan inhaled deeply, his chin lifting with pride. He glanced down into eyes so much like his own, and allowed his pride to show when he met his betrothed's gaze once more.

"This is Simone," he said simply. "My daughter."

And he knew, no matter who this woman was, he *would* find a way to make a peaceful future for them all.

Because he was *home*.

CHAPTER 4

For her first supper at An Torr, Mellie took great care in choosing her dress and her overall appearance. She knew she was playing a role here, and *had* been since the Queen's surprise announcement, though she was honest enough to admit, on the long days on the road—twice as many as necessary, because of that damned coach!—she'd allowed her disguise to slip.

But tonight she'd be meeting Lachlan's family and his people for the first time, and if she couldn't make a good impression now, it would make her mission only that much harder.

So she pulled out that same red silk gown she'd worn for the audience with the Queen, and had Brigit arrange her hair in the appealing—but slightly scandalous—waves down her back. She'd always had thick and heavy hair, and while it was easiest to wear in a simple braid, Mellie knew men—Lachlan in particular—found it appealing when she wore it loose.

Lachlan?

When had she started thinking of him by his first name?

Mayhap that horrible, wonderful moment, when she'd

stepped from the coach unassisted and had seen his face light up with pure *joy,* as he caught the little girl leaping into his arms.

Sainte Vierge!

Seeing the two of them together had done something to Mellie, *squeezed* something deep in her stomach she'd thought was long dead. The man's unabashed love and affection had been simultaneously uplifting and horrifying, as Mellie had struggled to understand the implications.

Bon Dieu, but she wished Rosa were here, to think through all the twists and turns.

Scowling, Mellie brushed Brigit away and took a deep breath. "I am ready," she whispered to her maid. Then, louder, to herself, "I *am ready.*"

I am an Angel, and I have a mission.

When she entered the great hall, Mellie was as charming and endearing as she could possibly be. She saw the appreciative looks the men cast her, and returned the hesitant smiles the women offered, with a confident and reassuring one of her own.

And despite *knowing* this was all part of a necessary manipulation, each smile, each welcome, made her steps lighter and her smile more genuine.

But it was Lachlan's reaction which affected her most strangely of all.

When he saw her, his gray eyes brightened in appreciation and a slow smile curved his lips upward, as his gaze raked over her, lingering on her breasts.

She *should've* been crowing with success, having prepared and presented herself for just such a reaction. But instead, his frank appraisal made her stomach flip over and her throat feel tighter.

"My lady," he said in a low voice, as he took her hand to help her up onto the dais beside him.

Mellie sucked in a breath, startled by the warmth which shot up her arm from the feel of her hand in his. His fingers tightened around hers—did he feel it too?—as he raised her hand to his lips.

Sainte Vierge!

And she'd thought it warm when he'd merely *touched* her?

The feel of his lips on her skin sent spikes of flames throughout her body, settling on her cheeks and deep inside her core.

Then, before she could fully understand her reaction, he turned to the gathered Frasers and lifted her hand in the air. With a booming voice and a pleasant smile, he addressed them.

"I am honored to present Lady Melisandre Lamond, whom Queen Elizabeth herself has arranged as my betrothed. Welcome and honor her as ye do me!"

A great roar of approval sprung from the gathered clan members and servants, cheering for their laird and the future of their clan. Mellie smiled and waved, playing the part of the overwhelmed bride far easier than she'd expected.

But when cries of "Kiss! Kiss!" rang out, she tried to tug her hand from his.

Lachlan turned then, his expression serious, even as his eyes sparkled with something she couldn't identify.

"Shall we, milady?"

"Nay, I—" Mellie was already shaking her head, before she remembered her reason for being there.

Her *purpose*.

The only way to learn this man's secrets was to seduce him, aye?

Which was exactly what she was good at.

Nay, 'tis what she was *excellent* at.

But Rosa's words tickled at the back of her mind as well: *Gain his trust, and his heart.*

Could she do that?

"Melisandre?" he prompted, tugging her gently to him.

Confused, not just at her own reaction to him, but at the look in his eyes, Mellie darted forward, and before she could lose her courage, or he could guess what she had planned, she brushed her lips across his.

The roar of their audience grew, and she pulled away, just in time to see his stunned expression, before she blushed and lifted her hand to nibble on a fingernail. Catching herself, she gripped her hands together, knowing she couldn't betray her nervousness.

"Well." He cleared his throat, and she peeked up at him in time to see his smile grow again as he shook his head. "Well, never let it be said ye donae ken how to please my people, Melisandre."

"Mellie," she blurted, then winced and met his eyes. "I mean, my friends call me Mellie."

His smile slowly faded, and his gray gaze skimmed her face, as if looking for the truth. "Are we friends then?" he asked quietly.

She was making a hash of things, was she not?

Mellie cleared her throat and raised her chin, forcing her hand away from her lips. "We are to be married."

He was silent for a long moment, before he nodded. "Aye, we are. And 'tis glad I am ye've made such an impression on the clan who will one day be yers. But for now…"

When he turned toward the head table, he didn't loosen his grip on her hand, but tugged her along with him as he introduced her.

"Ye ken Gillepatric, my father's advisor—"

"And yers, milord," the old man interrupted, then led with an ingratiating bow.

Lachlan grunted. "Indeed. And this is my mother, Isla."

Mellie smiled and curtsied to the older woman who was so intently studying her.

Finally, Isla nodded. "Marry this one quick, boy, before *she* gets away from ye too."

The comment was so startling and so unexpected, Mellie shot a glance at Lachlan, only to see his face flush.

From anger?

Embarrassment?

But before she could wonder any further at his reaction, he tugged her on. "This is Owen, my second-in-command and a good friend."

The big man held her hand a moment too long, but his wink and smile told her he was happy for his laird's upcoming marriage.

Clearing his throat, Lachlan glared at his friend, then gestured Mellie toward their seats. Before she could sit, however, he turned her to face him.

"And finally..." Reaching out his free arm, he wrapped it around the shoulders of the little girl—Mellie thought she was likely around six years old—who Lachlan had held in his arms in the courtyard when they'd arrived. "This is my daughter, Simone."

Mellie had known she was his child the moment she'd first laid eyes on her, and not just because of the affection he showed the lass.

While her blonde hair was lighter than her father's, she had the same gray eyes. Those, along with the smattering of freckles across her cheeks and nose, told Mellie she'd grow to be an incredibly beautiful woman, though she was already a very cute little girl.

Mellie's mind whirled, trying to remember everything Rosa had told her before she'd left. Lachlan Fraser had only been laird for a few years—two, right?—but had lived here with his family while his older brother had been laird.

Had Lachlan been married before?

Nay, surely Rosa would've mentioned it.

Mellie was aware there'd been a betrothal between him and some woman, but it had been broken years ago.

Simone had to be his natural daughter—a by-blow.

But the lass's curtsey was impeccable, which told Mellie Lachlan had done his duty by her, raising her correctly.

And it was clear he loved her, but who, and *where*, was her mother?

"Milady?"

Simone's hesitant prompt yanked Mellie's attention away from her whirling thoughts, and she glanced at Lachlan. The girl's father was watching her with a carefully neutral expression, as if wondering what she would say and do.

And in that moment, Mellie knew the truth: Though she was here to investigate—seduce and betray—Simone's father, she would *never* give this girl cause to think any less of herself, as Mellie had done for so long.

So she reached for the lass's hands, capturing them in hers, and made sure her smile was warm when she met Simone's eyes. "I am verra pleased to meet ye, Simone. I've heard so much about ye."

The girl's eyes flicked up to her father's, who couldn't hide the flash of surprise within them. But Mellie hadn't lied; she *had* heard the name Simone, several times from Lachlan himself, even if he hadn't bothered to explain who she was.

"Aye, Da likes to brag about me." Simone's smile was bright when she looked up at Mellie again. "Did he tell ye about the fish I caught?"

Unable to help the surprised burst of laughter which escaped her lips, Mellie shook her head. "He didnae. Ye'll have to tell me yerself."

Mellie shot a teasing grin his way, without a thought as to how easy it was to feel so carefree around him, only to realize he was glancing between the two of them with a look of concern.

Though he quickly recovered and offered a smile in return, Mellie had clearly seen the worry.

Amid the bustle and chaos of seating and serving, Mellie pondered his obvious unease.

Had he been worried she would reject the girl?

To his credit, the part she'd been playing—that of the cold, calculating lady-wife—likely would've made him think as much.

But did he really think so poorly of her, he expected she would needlessly hurt an innocent lass?

Why did that bother her so much?

She tried to think as if she were Rosa.

What did she know so far?

Well, Lachlan's attention to his daughter—however illegitimate she might be—proved he was a man who understood responsibility.

The delicious food she was enjoying said his household was well-run, and if he wasn't actually running it, then he was ensuring the position went to someone—his mother? The seneschal?—whom he trusted to get the job done.

The Frasers' cheers and excitement told Mellie he was well-loved and revered as the laird.

But it was the memory of what he'd said after that brief kiss—the kiss which she hadn't planned, and therefore, hadn't properly enjoyed—which gave her most pause.

He'd said he'd been glad she'd made an impression on the clan which would one day be hers. He believed this betrothal was real, which meant he thought he'd been introducing the future Lady Fraser to his people.

That explained his sudden attentiveness and honor when he'd presented her…he *wanted* her to be well-liked.

That, more than anything, told Mellie he cared for his clan's future and was a thoughtful and intelligent ruler.

Could that sort of man *also* be a traitor?

Sainte Vierge, but this is confusing.

On her left, Lady Isla Fraser kept up a running commentary on the dishes and the people around them, and Mellie tried her best to remember what she was saying, wondering how she would know what was important, and what was irrelevant, to her mission.

"This trout is well-prepared, but the fish is small. Ye can taste the difference, aye?"

Mellie murmured her agreement as she watched the servants doling out supper below.

Isla continued, "Now, when my Cameron was with us, he'd bring in the *biggest* trout the loch had ever seen! Why, even the monster herself couldn't eat all of these in one bite!"

Monster?

And who in the world was Cameron? Hadn't her husband's name been Michael?

God's Wounds, but for even a small portion of Rosa's memory!

"Aye, that lad was a born fisherman!" Isla continued fondly. "When he returns, he'll fill our stores for years, I'll wager."

From Mellie's other side came Lachlan's murmur, "Just ignore her, lass."

Mellie turned to see if he'd been speaking to her, just as he raised his voice so his mother could hear his next words.

"Ye ken Cameron's dead, Mother. Father Isaac says 'tis better for ye to spend yer breath praying for his soul, than hoping for his return."

"Bah!"

Mellie twisted back to see Isla glaring at her son, her eating knife brandished like a sword.

"Ye just *want* him to be dead. Ye and yer brothers—ye're all like that!" She jabbed the air in front of her with such vigor, Mellie leaned away. "Hamish and James and ye, ye're just jealous of him."

On her other side, Gillepatric was trying to quiet her, but Lachlan grunted quietly. "Jealous? Nay, Mother. Never."

The woman was clearly addled, stuck in the past with this Cameron person.

Hoping to distract Isla, Mellie blurted the first question which came to her mind. "Cameron, milady? I thought yer husband was Michael?"

Mayhap it was the right thing to ask, because Isla sighed happily as she sunk back into her seat and poked at her fish. "Aye, and Michael was a good leader, if a poor husband. Now *there* was a man who knew what was best for his clan!"

Did that mean she thought Lachlan—her own son!—was a poor leader?

Mellie frowned, but kept her attention on the woman, willing her to give more information. She was rewarded when the dowager launched into the history of the clan.

Unfortunately, she began over a hundred years ago, and her rambling not only took up most of the mealtime, but caused Mellie's attention to wander.

Finally, the woman got to the relevant history Mellie actually wanted to know about.

"Michael supported the Comyns, of course, rather than that upstart Bruce who took the throne after *murdering* poor John the Red."

At last!

Mellie leaned forward, only to be interrupted by Lachlan, who growled a warning.

"*Mother.*"

Isla waved away his irritation. "Posh! Yer brother Hamish

would've done something about that so-called *king*, had he lived that long."

"Mother, Red Comyn is *dead*. His line is *dead*. He will no' be King of Scotland. Robert the Bruce is the ruler we need, and he has done what *no other man* could in uniting this country and winning our freedom."

Bold, passionate words.

But had they been said merely for Mellie's benefit, or did Lachlan truly feel that way?

"Bah!" Isla pushed away her trencher. "Had poor James—as the second son—not been killed in that ridiculous war with the English, *he'd* be laird now. But Cameron—he's my youngest son, dear"—she said in an aside to Mellie—"*he'd* be the best of the lot of ye. He'd know *exactly* who to support in this—"

"Mother!" Slamming his fist down on the table, Lachlan made most of them jump. *"Enough.* My brother has been gone for fifteen years, and was too young to survive on his own when he left. Uncle Andrew followed him, but has found no sign of him, and now we've had no word from Andrew for years. *He's* likely dead too." Lachlan's chest heaved and his nostrils flared with the emotion he was trying to control. "Ye just need to accept these facts, Mother," he finished more gently.

For a long moment, Isla peered around Mellie at her son. Then her shoulders dropped and she sighed. Glancing down at her trencher, she said, "Ye may be right, lad."

Grunting again, Lachlan settled into his chair, but he didn't seem to be at any more ease.

Nay, he held himself as if he were...*ashamed*?

Ashamed at snapping at his mother?

On his other side, Simone was chattering about the fish she hoped to catch that week, and how it would rival her Uncle Cameron's catches she'd heard about. Lachlan would occasionally answer her, but Mellie kept quiet, content to listen and watch.

And wonder at the undercurrents of unrest here at An Torr.

~

Two days later, and Lachlan was still thinking about the way he'd snapped at his mother. The memory tasted sour in the back of his throat, and he recognized the sensation: shame.

The Frasers knew Mother hadn't been the same since Cameron had run off, and even though Lachlan wasn't sure if she knew *why* the lad had run, he did his best to treat her with sympathy. What he'd done the other night at the supper table had *not* been sympathetic...but mayhap it had finally needed to be said.

Mellie—and how strange, to think of her that way, although the name suited her—had been sent here by the Queen. Part of him wondered if she was the product of some sort of test.

The Crown needed to know he was loyal, aye, but was Mellie more than she seemed?

Aye, ye clot-heid, she is*! Remember the alleyway?*

The woman could take on the persona of a chilly noblewoman *or* a lusty temptress in the blink of an eye. She would be the perfect tool to use in testing his loyalty.

And on the very night of her arrival at An Torr, she'd had to hear his addled-headed mother spout treasonous drivel.

Would Mellie relay all of that to the Queen?

"Da, come on! Faster!"

Shaking himself from his thoughts, Lachlan smiled as he allowed his lass to tug him along the shore of the loch. "If I'd kenned ye wanted me to *run* to the baker's, I'd have told ye to go on without me."

"*Da!*" she whined and rolled her eyes. "Ye said ye were going this way anyhow."

He nodded along the shore to where the fishermen were mending their nets. "Nae farther than that."

"Well then, we can walk together— *Oh!*"

His daughter yanked to a stop, a frown on her face as she saw the figure strolling down the path leading from the village.

Mellie.

He'd recognize those curves anywhere.

"What's wrong?" he asked in a low voice.

Did Simone have reason to not want to meet up with Mellie?

But his worries were unfounded, because the lass swiftly pulled her hand from his and began to tug at her braid, smoothing the loose tendrils into order.

"What are ye doing?" he murmured, curious.

"Trying to look nicer for her." The small freckled face turned up to him. "Am I dirty? Lady Melisandre is always so pretty."

With a smile, he reached down and mussed her hair, earning a shriek from her as she ducked out from under his hand.

"*Da!*"

"Ye look beautiful, lass, and Lady Melisandre will think so too."

To his surprise, Simone flushed and looked down at her hands. "I want her to like me. I don' want her to—"

Alarmed at her serious tone, Lachlan dropped to his haunches and took her hands. "What is it, Simone?"

Gray eyes so like his own finally lifted and met his.

"I want her to like me, Da," she whispered, "so she doesnae go away like my mam did."

It was the fear in his daughter's expression which caused a fist to tighten around his heart.

"That wasnae yer fault," he whispered harshly, unable to say the words otherwise. "Yer mother…" He shook his head.

"Good morning!"

The cheerful call startled them both, but Lachlan was slow to rise, taking his daughter's hand back within his as he turned to his betrothed.

Mellie was radiant this morning, with the wind playing merry hell with her curls, and her tanned cheeks were kissed by the breeze.

This is how she'd look after a tumble, he was sure of it.

His cock jumped at the thought.

He cleared his throat. "Good morning, milady."

Mellie's smiled briefly at him, but quickly dropped her attention, and her smile, to Simone. "Are ye going fishing? I heard 'tis a good day for it."

Simone glanced up at him, as if looking for guidance, and he silently urged her to be herself.

Mayhap she understood, because she bit her lip, then answered Mellie hesitantly.

"I…donae ken, milady. The baker's younger son often lets me go out on the loch with him. I thought…" She swallowed. "Mayhap."

Rather than turn her nose up at the idea of a lass fishing, Mellie bent forward slightly. "I've heard stories of a *monster* who lives in the lake. Have ye ever seen her?"

Emboldened slightly, Simone shook her head, glanced up at her father, then raised her chin. " 'Tis just a tale, milady. Da says there's no such thing as monsters, and I believe him."

To his surprise, a cloud of sorrow passed briefly over

Mellie's expression, but she hid it by straightening and tucking a strand of hair behind her ear.

"Aye," she agreed, a little too cheerfully. "I cannae imagine a *real* monster living in such a wee lake anyhow."

Simone burst into laughter. "Wee? Loch Ness is *huge*, milady!"

Faking a nonchalant shrug, Mellie turned to look at the water, but peeked over her shoulder. "Not compared to where *I* grew up fishing."

His daughter's chuckles turned to a gasp so quickly, she almost choked. "What?" she sputtered. "*Ye* fished? Where?"

It was Mellie's turn to chuckle when she gestured Simone to stand by her side. "I'm a Lamond and grew up on the Firth of Clyde. Loch Ness is big, aye, but our loch south of here"—she pointed in that direction—"is even bigger. 'Tis because this is the Highlands, and the mountains determine where the lakes will be, aye?"

Simone was nodding eagerly, and when Mellie finished explaining, the lass grabbed hold of the woman's hand. "Ye are a Lowlander? And yer da let ye fish?"

"Well, ah…"

When Mellie lifted her fingernail to her lips and glanced over at Lachlan, he saw hesitation in her gaze and knew it was because of his daughter's question.

Well, no matter how or why she was here, he was pledged to marry her, which would make her Simone's mother of sorts. Let *her* figure out how to answer the question.

He raised one brow in challenge, letting her know she was on her own.

She took a deep breath, curled her hand into a fist, then shrugged.

Why did he feel as if she'd just accepted his challenge?

"Well, Simone"—she winked down at the girl—"my da

had strong feelings about things a lass should and shouldnae be allowed to do."

"Aye," his daughter agreed, and nodded sagely. "Grandmother is like that. But my da ignores her and lets me do what I please."

"No' quite true, ye wee hellion," Lachlan was quick to defend his parenting, stepping up beside the pair and scooping up his daughter. "I don' allow ye to paint mud on the walls. Or eat sweets before dinner."

Simone sighed and rolled her eyes. "Or practice with a sword bigger than my foot. Or stay up all night. Or climb that big tree in the bailey. Or go out on the loch all alone."

Chuckling, he tweaked her nose. " 'Tis glad I am ye remember the rules."

"*Da*!" she whined. Then, with a gasp, she twisted in his arms, so that one elbow was resting on his shoulder, and she was facing Mellie once more. "How'd ye go fishing then, milady?"

"*Mellie*," the woman corrected, and reached out to tap his daughter on her wee nose.

The motion seemed so natural, none of them recoiled; in fact, Simone giggled.

Not for the first time, Lachlan wondered what it would be like if he could find a wife who might cherish his lass as much as he did.

Could Melisandre Lamond, who seemed both haughty and earthy, be that woman?

Who was she really?

Simone was smiling, looking half in love already. "*Mellie*. Ye still went fishing?"

Mellie shrugged, lifting her fingernail to her lips in a motion he was sure was unconscious. "I…I confess I wasnae as experienced as ye seem to be. I can row a boat with the best of the fishermen though." A smile flitted across her face, as if remembering a specific instance. "But I went behind my da's back more than a few times."

Simone gasped and snaked her arm around Lachlan's neck for balance. "What did he do? Did he beat ye? My da says wicked men beat children, but I think he only says that so I don' cry too much over my punishments." She leaned in and lowered her voice, as if Lachlan wasn't standing right there with her attached to him. "When he takes away my bedtime story, I'm awfully sorry I was naughty."

Nodding seriously, Mellie was clearly hiding a smile. "I can imagine. He's a good father."

"Aye." Simone settled back. "He loves me verra much, and I love him. Did yer da love ye?"

If she'd thought she could avoid the topic, Mellie was mistaken. Still, she couldn't hide the flash of sorrow which crossed her face, before she turned back to the wind-swept waves of the loch.

"Mayhap no' as much as yer da loves ye, lass," she said with a sigh. "He's a powerful laird and believed—" She cut off whatever she'd been about to reveal, and glanced back at them with a fake smile. "He blamed my willfulness on my mother's blood, ye ken."

"Who's yer mother?"

Her false smile faded into a softer, more genuine one at Simone's question. "My mother was French, ye see. She was verra certain she kenned what was best for everyone, which drove my father mad." Her brow twitched as her grin turned wry. "Da always said I looked like her, but I donae ken 'twas praise, coming from him."

"Then she must have been verra beautiful." The words escaped Lachlan's lips before he could call them back—before he was even sure if he wanted to. But when he saw her flush, his cock twitched again.

"Thank ye," she whispered, acknowledging the compliment, even as she looked away.

Today she wore one of her court gowns, sewn to accentuate her body and show off those glorious tits of hers. She ought to look out of place, strolling along the shores of his loch, but somehow, she didn't. With her braid thrown over one shoulder, it was easy to let his eyes travel down over her curves.

She was dressed to accentuate her beauty, and he knew she used her looks to her advantage.

Curious about this woman he was to marry, Lachlan pressed on, "Surely 'tisnae the first time a man has called ye beautiful, lass."

There was a moments pause, before Mellie sucked in a breath and lifted her chin. Her blue eyes flashed at him for too brief a time, then she turned back away and looked off toward the village.

"Nay, of course not, milord. I am used to men telling me such all the time." Stiffly, she ran her hand down the side of her kirtle, caressing the curve of her hip. " 'Tis true after all, and is what a man values most."

Is that what she thought?

Lachlan frowned slightly, barely registering the way his daughter rested her head on his shoulder.

"A lass's worth is made up from far more than her appearance," he began, only to be cut off when she stepped away from them.

"Aye," she called out, not bothering to turn. "I ken all about a woman's worth, milord. Excuse me."

Holding his daughter in his arms, Lachlan stood and watched her march stiffly up the path back toward the village, wondering what in damnation was going on in her head.

His betrothed was a personal confidante of the Queen of

Scotland, sent here to test his loyalty. But she also pulled knives on cutpurses and had learned to row a boat without her father's permission.

What else would he learn about this intriguing young woman?

Who *was* she?

Because the more he knew about her, the less certain he was she was anything at all like Alice.

And if she wasn't like Alice—if she wasn't selfish and heartless, like the other ladies he'd known, interested only in bettering their station in life—then mayhap their future together could be happier than he'd once expected.

Mayhap.

CHAPTER 5

"The poor lad was only twelve when he left."

Mellie frowned down at the piece of parchment, which was still blank. She'd pushed the small table up against the open window for better light, but it hadn't helped; she still had nothing to write.

Which is why she'd cornered Brigit when the girl had brought luncheon and demanded gossip.

"This is Cameron?" she muttered distractedly, trying to focus on the story the maid was telling her about a lad running off years ago.

"Aye, the wee thing left in the middle of winter too, if ye can believe it. Are ye going to eat this bread?"

With a sigh, Mellie tossed down the stylus and leaned back in the chair. "Nay, enjoy it."

Her stomach was still churning at her inability to make a report to Charlotte.

The *how* wasn't that difficult; with Brigit on her side, she could send the girl into the village, or mayhap farther, to send the letter.

But the *what* was proving more difficult.

After almost a sennight here at An Torr, she had absolutely nothing to report.

A nearly full sennight had been spent making herself useful around the keep, in an attempt to gain more knowledge of her *betrothed*.

A sennight spent embroidering with his mother, or discussing menus with the cook, or learning about the clan's history from Martin, the old seneschal.

A sennight sitting beside Lachlan on the dais each evening, pretending—as he was—to be happy about this betrothal, while the whole time, she wanted to squirm with confusion and frustration.

She was failing her mission, but every moment spent with Lachlan—any time they touched, whether on accident or otherwise—made her insides warm. She remembered the brief kiss she'd given him her first evening here, when his clan members had cajoled them into it...and wasn't sure if she wanted more, or wanted to forget that feeling altogether.

Because she'd been unable to find any evidence Lachlan was guilty of treason, or was in *any* way associated with the Red Hand. In fact, everyone she spoke to raved about Lachlan's honor, integrity and loyalty.

And now, even the gossip was failing her!

She sighed and forced herself to concentrate on Brigit's story about Cameron..

"Is there any evidence the lad is dead?" Mellie asked, as she lifted her fingernail to gnaw at it.

Her maid shook her head enthusiastically, her eyes bright with excitement from sharing gossip, and waited until she'd swallowed the bread before answering. "Nay! But there's been nae word from him for so long, most assume the poor lad perished soon after leaving. The laird's uncle—his father's younger brother—left soon after to search for him, but found nae sign of him!"

Nodding, Mellie remembered what she'd heard that first day from Lachlan and his mother. "And now nae one's heard from the uncle either?"

"Aye, Andrew is his name."

How was this helpful?

Mellie squeezed her eyes shut and tried to think like Rosa.

The youngest brother would've left when Michael Fraser, Lachlan's father, was still laird.

Was it possible the man's treason had something to do with his disappearance?

Had he truly left on his own?

"Does anyone know *why* the lad ran off?" Mellie asked her maid.

If possible, Brigit's eyes grew even wider as she scooched around the table to plop herself in the seat across from Mellie, directly in front of the window. She then planted her elbows on the table and leaned forward, waving a hunk of cheese around as she gestured excitedly.

" 'Tis shocking really! The auld laird and lady Isla had four sons, aye? The eldest was Hamish, who became laird after his father passed."

Mellie nodded, remembering this from Rosa's briefing before she'd left Scone.

The maid lowered her voice. "Hamish was already wed, ye see, but never fathered any children. Several people are convinced he and his wife—they'd been betrothed since birth—never consummated their marriage. 'Tis said he had…*unnatural* tendencies."

Frowning, Mellie chewed furiously at her nail. No matter what the societal norm was, she knew there were those—both men *and* women—who had other desires. "But why would—"

But Brigit interrupted. *"With children."*

Mellie sucked in a gasp, and her maid nodded, their shared disgust reflecting in each other's eyes. Her stomach churned.

"With lads?" she whispered, dropping her hand to the table, where it curled into a fist.

But the other woman shrugged. "Likely so, according to the stories I've heard. So nae one was completely surprised when wee Cameron ran off; if his older brother was preying on him, what other choice did he have? And if his parents kenned of Hamish's habits, they surely made nae great effort to stop him."

"But now he's dead," Mellie confirmed in a harsh whisper.

Brigit nodded. "Aye. A training accident, 'tis said." She leaned in once more. "But *I* heard the warrior who did it had a son of only ten winters, and the laird had been spending time with the lad prior to the *accident*."

"May he burn in hell," Mellie spat, then crossed herself. *Sainte Vierge!*

Hamish had been dead for over two years now, and his soul had already been judged and sentenced, but she felt it couldn't hurt to be sure.

However horrifying the previous laird had been, none of this information helped her with the current laird.

"And Lachlan became laird because the second son—what was his name…James?—was already dead?"

Brigit nodded. "Aye. He lost his life at Loudon Hill against the English," she told Mellie, then took another bite of cheese.

"So the Frasers were still loyal enough to the crown to send warriors to fight for the cause, at least," Mellie murmured, staring down at her blank report to Charlotte. It didn't prove anything, but it was a start.

Picking up the stylus, she wrote: ***Frasers fought for Robert at Loudon Hill.***

It was better than nothing, and mayhap would lend credence to the theory not all of the Frasers supported the Comyns.

Or mayhap it only meant they wanted a Comyn on the throne, and would fight for Scotland against the English to ensure that would one day happen.

She sighed, irritation warring with worry in her gut. She was failing Queen Elizabeth by not finding evidence of Lachlan's guilt.

Yet…why did that make her feel so much relief and give her such *hope*?

Sainte Vierge!

Was it possible she didn't *want* to find evidence linking Lachlan to the traitorous attempt on Elizabeth's life?

Was it possible she wanted to believe him innocent?

With a groan, she dropped her head into her hands.

After a sennight here at An Torr, the Frasers' belief in their laird was starting to rub off on her!

"Brigit," she mumbled from between her hands, "have ye heard *aught* to indicate Lachlan isn't the paragon of leadership he seems to be?"

When her maid took a moment to answer, Mellie peeked from between her fingers to see the other woman frowning thoughtfully. But finally, she shook her head.

"Nay, milady. He's good for the clan, and everyone seems to adore him. I havenae heard anything about his loyalties being suspect either. I heard what he said at the welcome dinner, and everyone says he's an honorable supporter of the Bruce."

Merde!

Was it possible their theory about him was wrong?

Mellie rubbed at her forehead, trying to remember everything Rosa had argued—for and against the Frasers—since the assassination attempt. Of course, that was a fortnight ago.

Was Court back at the palace yet with more news?

Mellie forced herself to think like Rosa once more.

What else would be relevant to this investigation?

"Simone!" she blurted, then rested her chin on her hands, staring at her maid. "Surely ye have some gossip about her? Who her mother was?"

In the previous week's discussions, not one person had mentioned any of Lachlan's mistresses, and the man hadn't snuck off from his duties to his clan to secretly visit his leman, at least as far as Mellie knew.

So who was she?

Brigit shrugged, then nibbled at the cheese once more. "The laird was betrothed once before."

Aye, Mellie knew this. Rosa had told her—

She sucked in a sudden breath.

"He sired a child with his betrothed?" It wasn't unheard of, but why wouldn't he have just married the woman, once she told him of her state? Unless… "He wanted to see if the bairn survived, if she was a good mother."

The knowledge, the *certainty*, settled into her stomach like a rock.

Bon Dieu! He'd waited until the bairn was born before deciding about the mother. But Simone was a healthy child. Unless…

"Was it because she's a lass, and no' an heir?" Shaking her head, Mellie pushed herself to her feet, but kept a tight grip on the table with both hands. She wasn't sure she could stand otherwise. "Nae matter how loved Simone is, she'll never be what he *needs*. And that's—"

Shaking her head, she stumbled away, reaching for a bed post to catch herself, as memories from her own past came back to haunt her.

—to be expected.

—a man's right.

Ye cannae expect a powerful laird to still marry a failure like ye.

The harsh words spoken by her father, her confessor, and even a few others, sliced open all the scarred-over wounds covering her heart, and ignited the once-smoldering embers of pain in her stomach into a roaring flame once more.

Sainte Vierge!

Lachlan was no better than her own betrothed had been, may God forgive them both!

She clutched her stomach, fighting back tears, as she glared at the door where she imagined Lachlan to be currently standing.

From the window seat, Brigit said in a small voice, "I donae ken *why* the betrothal was broken, milady, but I ken she went home to her family not long after the birth, and entered into another marriage the following spring."

With a growl—where had that come from?—she forced herself to straighten. Her shoulders went back, her breasts thrust forward, and her jaw clenched with determination and anger.

Lachlan *was* a bastard, a wicked man indeed. And if he could treat an innocent woman that way—banishing her and keeping her from any contact with her own bairn —then Mellie could believe he was guilty of treason too.

And she *would* find evidence, and possibly from his very own lips!

Rosa had urged her to gain his trust, without using her seduction techniques, but when had that ever worked for her before?

Nay, there was only one thing Mellie was good at—one thing she was good *for*—and she intended to use it to the very best of her ability.

Lord help him if he thought he could resist her.

And if she had to fuck every single one of his secrets out of him, she would.

"Brigit," she commanded, in a low voice. When the maid scrambled out of the seat to stand, wide-eyed before her, Mellie nodded. "Fetch my red gown. I need to visit *my betrothed.*"

As she lifted her fingers to her hair to pull out the pins her maid had carefully inserted that morning, Mellie's eyes narrowed determinedly.

She *would* have a report for Charlotte, along with all the evidence the Angels needed to condemn Lachlan Fraser.

~

"Catch 'im! Get 'im"

The shouts came from behind Lachlan, where he walked alone, having fallen behind the other men on their return from the training fields, because he was distracted. His thoughts were on Mellie, and the way she'd been at dinner last night—at times flirtatious, other times, rather standoffish. It also seemed to him as if she weren't quite sure of her role at An Torr.

Though to be honest, her dueling personas have confused *him*, ever since the moment he'd realized she wasn't the knife-wielding wench he'd thought her to be, and was, in reality, a lady of the royal court.

Wasn't she?

Hell, he didn't know, and mayhap she didn't either.

"Laird! Laird, catch 'im!"

This time, Lachlan turned, and it was a damned good thing he did.

Three lads were barreling right toward him—he recognized one of the lads as young Ian from the stables—and were shaking sticks and rakes, and running like the fires of hell were behind them.

Nay, not *behind* them.

Something caught his attention, and he realized the lads appeared to be chasing a small, brown, squealing…

Piglet?

"Get 'im, Laird!"

Lachlan's brows shot up, but he did what any good laird would do; he spread his legs, stuck out his arms to either side, and tried to catch the terrified animal.

The piglet ran right through his open legs.

A chorus of groans and shouts went up from the lads, and Lachlan had to reach out to steady one—Thomas's son?—as they ran by.

"Come on, Laird!" the lad shouted, squirming to struggle out of Lachlan's grip. "He's the last one of the lot who escaped!"

Chuckling now, Lachlan freed the boy to run off toward the commotion, then stuck two fingers in his mouth. The ear-piercing whistle was one his men all recognized, and he was pleased to see more than a few of them instinctively reach for their swords as they turned toward him.

Battle-hardened warriors or nay, they were about to meet a *real* challenge.

"Catch him, men!" Lachlan bellowed, pointing to the piglet, who was just about to hit the wall of Fraser muscle, before it turned, squealing, and headed straight for the curtain wall.

But the Fraser warriors had trained together for years and knew how to work in tandem. Some moved left, some moved right, some filled in the middle, and soon there was a ring of hollering, laughing men moving inward toward the frightened animal.

Back legs frantically pedaling, the piglet changed directions once more, shooting out from under Owen's lunge, and running back toward the lads. Young Ian dove, arms outstretched, but missed completely, coming up spitting mud and grass.

If the men hadn't all been laughing before, they certainly were now.

The next three minutes were frantic ones, calling encouragement and challenges to one another as the wee, squealing animal darted from one side of the closing circle to the other, looking for a way out.

It was a surprising amount of fun.

Finally, his man Angus lifted his arms and jumped forward, bellowing at the poor creature. He was hairy enough, the piglet likely thought he was being attacked by a bear, and in terror, it turned completely about on only one front leg.

As the piglet hurtled, screaming across the circle toward Lachlan, the laird did the only thing he *could* do...

Pushing his sword out of his way, he dropped to one knee and thrust out his leg to block the piglet's charge, then threw the bulk of his upper body down onto the poor creature.

Lachlan could feel the animal squirming to escape underneath him, so he quickly tore off his shirt and wrapped the piglet securely inside the cloth.

Still laughing, he rolled to his feet and thrust the squirming bundle at young Ian, who grinned through the muddy mask on his face, and waved as he ran off.

"Always kenned ye were nimble, Laird!" Thomas cried, as he slapped Lachlan's shoulder.

Angus did the same, though nearly felling Lachlan with his heavy blow. "The pig-catcher of the Frasers is what they'll call ye!"

Laughter and jokes flew back and forth, and Lachlan found himself reveling in the camaraderie.

"I cannae recall the last time I've had so much fun," he called out, then gave a mischievous wink, and added, "without my sword."

"Nay, milord," Owen shot back, lewdly grabbing at his crotch, "Ye need yer sword for the best kinds of fun!"

The raucous laughter rose again, and Lachlan slapped more than a few of his friends on the shoulder, before they began to disperse.

"If ye plan things right, milord, ye might be able to get in a wee bit of sword practice right now!"

Before Lachlan could ask Owen what he meant, his friend pointed upward. Lachlan followed his finger, then raised a brow.

There, standing on the walk and staring down at their antics, without a hint of what she thought of them showing on her face, was his betrothed.

Feeling bold after his battle with the piglet, Lachlan stepped away from the crowd and sketched a deep courtly bow. It was all the more ridiculous, being that he was shirtless, covered in dried sweat and the stink of pig, but if she were planning on living at An Torr, she'd have to get used to their simple way of life.

When he rose, he met her eyes. Her neutral expression never changed, but she did hold his gaze for a long while.

She's wearing that red gown again.

The one she wore at court, the first time he'd realized who she was. The one she wore her first dinner here at An Torr.

The one which did amazing things to her curves, and made him want to taste her skin.

After a long moment, she lifted her hand and stretched it out toward him…then beckoned.

God's Blood!

His knees went all tingly.

Then Mellie turned away, but after only a few steps, she threw a little smile over her shoulder, and Lachlan knew he'd follow her anywhere.

But first, to the well to wash.

Then he'd track her down and...and...

Sighing, he shook his head.

He'd track her down, and then what?

Demand to know the real Melisandre?

Demand to know why she was *really* there?

Demand to know *why* she'd saved him that day in the alleyway?

Mayhap he'd be able to think better when he was cleaner.

He didn't.

Ten minutes later, he was pushing his hand through his wet hair as he took the steps to the keep three at a time. His thoughts were still jumbled, and the bucket of cold water he'd poured over his head hadn't helped sort his thoughts one bit.

He was mostly still thinking about that smile his betrothed had sent him after she'd beckoned him to her. And his cock was proof of those thoughts.

"Ah, excellent timing, milord!"

Lachlan's temper was so high, his desires so frustrated, that when Gillepatric stopped him on his way across the great hall, he almost snapped at the older man. No matter how devoted he was to his clan's future, there were limits to a man's geniality! And when his cock was rock-hard, and there was a damnably confusing woman upstairs, waiting to—

Nay.

He shook his head and took a deep breath, forcing himself to give a polite nod to his father's advisor. He couldn't allow thoughts of Mellie to jeopardize everything he'd worked so hard to build within the Fraser clan.

"Aye, Gillepatric? Is something amiss?"

"Oh, naught, naught, lad!" The older man was smiling widely over his beard. "I just wanted to inform ye, yer mother has gotten it into her head to visit Scone. I'll escort her o' course, and I thought we might pay our respects at the palace while we're there, to assure Her Majesty ye are well settled with yer betrothed."

Lachlan nodded distractedly, his attention only on climbing the stairway leading up to his chambers and finding a dry—*non-piglet-scented*—shirt. "Fine, fine. Are ye sure ye're up to traveling again so soon?"

The advisor chuckled. "I'm auld, but there's still plenty of life left in these bones, lad!" He slapped his stomach. "And plenty of schemes in this mind."

When he tapped the side of his head and winked at Lachlan, the younger man frowned slightly.

Schemes?

And now he thought about it, just *why* exactly was Gillepatric so anxious to go off traveling with Lachlan's mother?

"I can send some of her maids with her, Gillepatric, so ye are no' obligated—"

"Now, now." The older man tsked as he shook his head, then winked again. "Just because yer mother is a wee bit aulder, doesnae mean she doesnae have her own desires and kens her own mind. If she wants to travel with a fit, kind, aulder man, then who are ye to say differently?"

"For one, I'm her son—"

But when Gillepatric winked again, Lachlan finally realized what in damnation the man was trying to tell him, and nearly blanched.

Was Lachlan's father's advisor interested in a liaison with *Mother*?

Lachlan swallowed. "Aye. Um...fine." He cleared his

throat and shook his head, praying for God to release him from the disturbing mental images now assaulting him. "Ye're right. She *is* her own woman, and she does ken her own mind"—*at least, she kens her own mind when she isn't hanging off the edge into complete and total madness*—"but ye are to take enough men to ensure her safety."

Gillepatric bowed deeply, his smile still in place, and Lachlan backed away from the all-around disturbing encounter.

Sucking in a deep breath, he turned away and forced himself to maintain his normal saunter, but as soon as he was out of sight of the advisor, his legs took on a mind of their own and rushed him toward his chambers.

His erection had immediately abated when—*dear Lord, help me!*—he realized his mother—

When he realized Gillepatric—

Nay!

Stop thinking about it, ye clot-heid!

Lachlan repeated the words, *Clean shirt. Clean shirt. Clean shirt*, in his mind as he made his way to his chambers. He would get that damned shirt first, just as he'd planned, but then he was going to track down that lady in red of his and get some answers, once and for all.

But the desire he'd felt earlier, which had so quickly disappeared when—

Nay!

The earlier desire came slamming back, though with even more intensity, when he pushed open his door.

She was there, standing in front of his chamber window so the afternoon light silhouetted her like some kind of...*angel*.

Her hair hung loose and freely down her back and flowed over her shoulders. A golden halo, streaked with red, that his fingers itched to run through.

And that blasted crimson gown…!

Lachlan swallowed the lump in his throat, then shut the door behind him.

God help him, but that gown!

"Lachlan," she said, in a throaty, seductive tone of voice, and under his kilt, his cock hardened even more.

Saints preserve him, he'd thought her lovely before, but *now*?

Now, when she used those too-wide, too-sensual lips to send that enticing, flirtatious smile in his direction, she was absolutely *exquisite*.

"Mellie," he managed to rasp out, "what are ye doing here?"

He knew what he *wanted* her to be doing, but also knew it was unlikely to happen.

Still giving him that wicked smile, she lifted her hand, and he only then saw the dry shirt dangling from her delicate fingers. "I thought to help ye, husband-to-be."

Closing his eyes briefly, Lachlan breathed a silent prayer for strength.

But when he opened them again, she was *there*, right in front of him.

He could reach out and touch her.

Hold her.

Taste her!

They were betrothed, so why *shouldn't* he be allowed to touch her, hold her…*taste* her,, at least a few times before the ceremony?

"Let me help ye dress, Lachlan," she said, in that husky voice, which seemed to be directly linked to the tip of his cock, judging from the way it jumped again.

"I can—" He shook his head and forced himself to think properly, as he took the shirt from her. "I can dress myself."

"Can ye?"

"Aye, woman," he ground out.

To his chagrin, her tongue darted out across her lower lip, making it glisten.

Did she do that on purpose, to tease him?

"I want to ken all about ye, Lachlan," she said, in that same arousing voice. "I want to be useful to ye, to learn everything I can. I can *help* ye. Let me ken yer secrets."

It was an odd request, and as soon as he could think rationally, Lachlan was sure he'd be able to figure out why. But right now...

He shook his head once more. "I have nae secrets," he managed. "I am a simple man—"

And then she was in his arms.

He wasn't sure how it happened—had she really moved so quickly?—but one moment she was in front of him, then the next moment she had her arms around his neck, her fingers twisting in the hair at the base, her lips stretching up toward his.

And Lachlan stopped thinking.

On her first night here at An Torr, she'd kissed him in front of his people. He'd be damned if he'd let *her* kiss *him* again.

Nay, this time *he'd* be the one doing the kissing.

Instinctively, his hands reached for her waist to hold her steady as he met her lips midway. When they melted against his, he dragged his palms up each side of her torso, then slid one arm around her back to hold her in place as he kissed her.

Her lips parted under his, and she let out a little moan, which made his pulse pound and his cock strain forward.

Could she feel it under his kilt, pressed against her hip like that?

Did she know what it meant?

And then she wriggled against him, making a sexy little

noise of encouragement, and Lachlan wondered if he'd died and gone to Heaven. Not only did she obviously *know*, but she was *encouraging* it.

His free hand flexed, stretching out his fingers, until they brushed against the underside of one of her breasts, and when she didn't pull away, he groaned deep in his throat.

He hadn't been this close to spilling against his kilt since he was a lad!

God's Wounds, this kiss was undoing him.

With a gasp, he pulled away, but didn't overlook the way her grip on his shoulders seemed to tighten.

Was she as affected as he was?

But as his breathing returned to normal, so did his reason, and he met her gaze. He'd been about to apologize—both for his actions, and for the very clear indication of his arousal still pressed against her—but something in her eyes stopped him.

Those blue pools weren't glazed with passion the way he'd assumed. They weren't confused, or even offended, by his kiss.

Nay. They were…calculating.

He swallowed, trying to make sense of what he was seeing. He'd thought her to be like Alice, but even Alice—who hadn't been a virgin when she'd given herself to him—hadn't once ever looked at him in this way.

What in damnation was Mellie thinking?

His hand still rested against the underside of her breast. As he moved it, he tried for a smile, but knew it came out rather weakly. "Mellie…" he began.

Who knows how he would've finished, had she not dropped her hands away from his shoulders at that moment, and shifted her weight back.

He thought she was about to throw herself away from him, and braced himself to catch her if she needed his help.

What he *didn't* expect was her to drag her hands to his forearms, her palms sending sparks into his stomach as they caressed his bare skin.

And then, in one swift movement, she sank to the floor in a crouch before him.

What in God's sacred name...?

She settled on her knees and released one of his arms. While his mind was still whirling, she reached for the bottom of his plaid and lifted it.

It wasn't until the cooler air brushed against his bollocks that he realized what she was doing, and he made a strangled noise somewhere between denial and a gasp.

In less than a heartbeat, his body and his mind warred.

He wanted this; God knew he'd been *dreaming* of her lips on him often enough.

But he'd seen the look in her eyes after their kiss, and Lachlan knew this was no act of passion. This was…something else.

That realization made his decision for him.

He abruptly dropped to one knee, effectively blocking her, just as Mellie reached for his cock. She reared back, blinking in confusion, as he took hold of her shoulders in a gentle, but firm, grip.

"What—" God help him, but he couldn't seem to make his voice work properly. "Why are ye doing this, Mellie?" he managed to ask.

She sank back on her haunches, her eyes showing her confusion…but also a haunted look.

"I… I thought ye might like it if I…"

Her golden curls bounced when she shook her head, but Lachlan wasn't thinking of what they'd feel like—not anymore. Instead, he watched her wrap one arm around herself and lift her thumbnail to her teeth, and he felt as if he were looking at someone else entirely. A lass who was confused and worried, who wasn't sure about his reaction, and was uncertain if he was angry with her or not.

Her troubled countenance, more than anything else, effectively and thoroughly cooled his ardor.

"Lass," he began, in a rough whisper, his thumbs making little circles on her shoulders because he couldn't seem to release her just yet. "Aye, I *would* like it, as would any man, but *why* would ye do it? Why now?"

A flush stole up her sun-kissed cheeks, and she looked away, staring at the floorboards beside his knee.

Had that been a flash of shame he'd seen in her gaze?

What had she been saying to him before their kiss?

Something about getting to know him?

Learning his secrets?

Not for the first time, Lachlan wondered if that was why she was really there.

Had Queen Elizabeth betrothed her to him, just for the purpose of discovering his secrets?

To learn all she could about him?

To discover if he was a traitor?

And was that why she'd kissed him like that?

Why she'd been willing to sink to her knees, to take him in her lush mouth?

Why she'd been willing to submit herself to him as she had, offering her body for him to use?

He nearly groaned aloud.

"Mellie…" He shook his head, squeezing his eyes shut as his thoughts whirled. "Mellie," he repeated, in a harsh whisper.

"Aye, *milord*?"

When he opened his eyes, she was watching him, her expression carefully neutral.

"Mellie, ye don' have to do this. Ye don' have to—to—*offer* yerself."

Her chin rose as her hand fell away from her lips. "I want to."

It was a lie. He could see it easily in her blue eyes.

His grip on her shoulders tightened. "Ye do no' need to. I will tell ye whatever ye need to ken. The truth."

He meant it, and he could see she was affected by his word. Her hand twitched, as if she wanted to lift her nail to nibble on it once more, but she held herself back.

As she had been this whole time. Since he'd met her—there in that alley, and then again in the Queen's court—she'd been holding her true self back. He had no idea who she *truly* was.

"The truth?" she repeated, lifting her chin with a hint of that haughty air he'd seen at the Queen's side.

"Aye."

He lifted one hand from her shoulder and touched her cheek. When she didn't flinch away, he skimmed his fingertips across her skin, toward her ear, tucking an errant curl safely out of the way.

"Always," he whispered.

"Well, *my* truth is, Lachlan, that I *wanted* to taste ye." Her chin jutted mulishly, but there were tears gathering in her blue eyes. "What do ye have to say about that? A betrothed, who is little more than a common whore—"

"Nay."

He knew his voice was hard when he cut her off, but he didn't care. She needed to know her own worth.

He dropped his other hand from her shoulder, but his fingertips remained on her cheek.

"There is nothing *common* about ye, Melisandre Lamond. Ye might understand passion, but that only makes ye more intriguing. What ye were doing"—he winced as he tried to find the words to explain—"ye donae have to do that. No' for me."

"I…" It was her turn to shake her head, sending her curls bouncing. "I donae—"

When she cut herself off with a noise which sounded suspiciously like a sob, Lachlan moved his fingers to her chin to hold her gaze, and to keep from losing her.

"Mellie," he began softly, "ye are worth more than just giving a man pleasure."

A shudder passed through her as her eyes widened in shock at his words.

Why?

Had no one said that to her before?

When she tried to shake her head again, he held her in place with a gentle pressure, and countered her denial with a slow nod of his own.

"Ye are worth more than this."

With a sob, she broke away from him by throwing herself backward, before scrambling to her feet. The silk gown tangled in her legs, but she didn't allow that to stop her.

Instead, she muffled her sobs with her palm, and when she was steadily back on her feet, she paused in her flight to look down at him.

Her shoulders were heaving and tears streamed down her cheeks. The look in her vivid blue eyes was almost wild—confused, frantic, frightened—as she met his gaze.

Then, with another muffled sob, she whirled and bolted for the door.

Lachlan knelt there on the floor of his chambers, his cock softening beneath his kilt, and cursed himself for a fool.

Who in all of Creation *was* she?

CHAPTER 6

Mellie stared down at the parchment resting between her two hands. It was her report to Charlotte, and it was still blank.

In the days since she'd kissed Lachlan—then tried to do *other* things—she'd paced her room, trying to make sense of what she'd learned. She'd even taken her suppers in her chambers, alone, claiming a headache.

Likely *he'd* known the truth, but she was far too embarrassed to face him.

Not after he'd rejected her so...so...*nicely.*

Like a true gentleman.

She took a deep breath and rolled her head from side to side.

What *did* she know about him?

Well, other than Brigit's gossip, she was no closer to finding the truth about his loyalties, or the likelihood of him committing treason.

But she was learning more and more about Lachlan, the man, wasn't she?

She knew he was a good leader, one who valued peace and his clan's prosperous future.

She knew he wasn't afraid of hard work, and in fact, seemed to prefer it to sitting in his solar with his seneschal.

She knew all that hard work had built a glorious set of shoulders, and a chest she wanted to *lick*. The man was well-built, and the sight of his strong arms alone could make her—

Focus.

With a sigh, she picked up the parchment, rolled it, then set it down and smoothed it back out again, all the while watching the way her hands moved.

What *else* did she know about Lachlan?

He was a good father and loved his daughter deeply.

He'd once been betrothed, but when the poor woman had given him a daughter instead of a son, he'd sent her away.

He was the only man to ever look her in the eyes and tell her she was worth more than the pleasure she could bring him.

He was the only man who'd rejected her seduction, despite the fact she could clearly feel his need and desire.

He was the only man who'd ever held her tenderly and told her she was worth *more*.

With a groan, Mellie dropped her head into her hands, willing her tears not to fall. For one thing, she'd cried enough over the last days. For another, she didn't want to have to clean the parchment if she spilled her tears all over it.

Sainte Vierge!

She'd offered herself to him—had gotten *down on her knees* for him!—and he'd rejected her in the most heart-wrenching, the most beautiful, way possible.

That didn't sound like the actions of a man who had banished his first betrothed, then kept her from her own daughter, did it?

Mellie's eyes flashed open. Through her fingers, she stared down at the blank report in front of her.

Suddenly, Lachlan's past, his loyalties, seemed to fade in the background. Although her mission here at An Torr was to determine if he was behind the assassination attempt, she found herself thinking of Rosa's advice instead.

Gain his trust, and his heart.

She couldn't do all of that, nay. But mayhap…

Mayhap if she could find the truth of *who he was*, then mayhap she'd find the truth of his actions.

I will tell ye whatever ye need to ken.

He'd said that yesterday, after he'd dropped to his knees in front of her and taken her in his arms. Her heart had been so torn, she hadn't been paying attention, but now?

She *couldn't* come right out and ask him if he was behind the assassination attempt, could she?

He'd surely say no, so could she trust it was the truth?

Gain his trust.

Nay.

First, he had to gain *hers*.

"Lady Mellie?"

The small voice from the door caused Mellie to gasp and spin around in surprise. She caught herself attempting to hide the parchment behind her back, before remembering it was blank.

Wee Simone was peaking around the doorframe, but when she found she now had Mellie's attention, her eyes lit up, and she stepped into the room. "I'm sorry for bothering ye, Lady Mellie, but the door was ajar. Are ye still sick?"

"I—" Mellie shook her head, flustered.

She'd left the door ajar?

Or had someone else opened it and been peeking in on her?

Was life at An Torr as idyllic as it seemed, or was she just too used to thinking as an Angel and seeing conspiracies everywhere she looked?

"I am better now, thank ye."

Nodding, Simone took another few steps into the room. "Da said ye werenae feeling well yesterday eve, and when I came to see ye this morning, yer door was closed." She looked around the room, her eyes lingering on the gowns Brigit had hung on hooks along the wall. " 'Tis my favorite room in the keep, ye ken."

One of Mellie's brows rose, as she scooted a chair around to face the girl, then sat. "I didnae ken that. Even more so than yer nursery?"

The wee lass made a face as she crossed to the bed. "Ella is my nursemaid, and she's auld an' boring. My bed there is comfortable enough, I guess." She leaned both hands and her weight on the mattress. "But I was born here in this bed, ye ken. That's what Da tells me."

Slowly, Mellie stood, both brows raised high this time, as she looked around the chamber. It was An Torr's nicest guest chamber, and had likely belonged to the ladies of the keep in the past. It wasn't hard to believe Lachlan's first betrothed had been assigned this room as well.

And had birthed her child here.

Had she done so, knowing the bairn would be loved and accepted by the father? And had she known, even then, she wouldn't have a place in her daughter's life?

Unconsciously, one of Mellie's fingers rose to her lips as she tried to make sense of it all.

Lachlan *did* love and accept his daughter, there was no question about that. But why had he sent Simone's mother away? And could a man who would do that also betray his King?

She needed more information, if she was to determine the truth about Lachlan Fraser.

And the wee lass in front of her may just be the source she needed.

"I *am* feeling much better, Simone. Would ye like to take a walk with me?"

A look of guilt flashed across the lass's face. "Um..."

"Ah. Does Ella, yer nursemaid, no' ken where ye are? Will she be cross if ye—"

"Nay!" The little girl clasped her hands in front of her and shifted her weight from one tiny foot to the other. "Actually, she's napping. She's quite auld, ye ken." Peeking up at Mellie, the lass offered a hesitant smile. "I was gonna go down to the loch, but then I thought mayhap..."

When she trailed off, Mellie cocked her head to one side. "Aye?"

"I thought mayhap"—the little girl shrugged, then took a deep breath and said, all in one breath—"ye-might-want-to-go-fishing-with-me-Lady-Mellie-but-ye-don'-have-to-if-ye-don'-want-to-but-would-ye-please?"

Mellie's lips curved upward. This was the perfect opportunity for her to possibly learn more details, but that hadn't been her first thought.

Nay, when the lass invited her, Mellie's first thought had been one of excitement at the chance to spend time with Simone.

"I think that sounds like a wonderful idea, Simone. But ye have to do me a favor."

The wee lass's face lit with excitement, her gray eyes sparkling. "Aye? Anything!"

Mellie offered her hand, and when Simone took it, she squeezed the little girl's hand gently.

"Call me Mellie."

~

"Milord! Milord, I cannae find wee Simone!"

Lachlan grunted as he hoisted the stone he was building into place, then turned toward the call as he wiped his dusty hands on his plaid.

His daughter's elderly nursemaid was waddling across the yard, appearing cross and agitated. He stifled his sigh and raised his hand to let her know he'd heard her.

"We can handle the rest of this, milord," said Owen, who was working beside him.

They'd been at the wall repairs since early that morning, and Lachlan reveled in the feel of his muscles straining, and the way his back ached. *Anything* was welcome which might help wipe away the memory of Mellie on her knees, reaching for his cock—

He cleared his throat. "Ye're sure?"

His best friend, and second-in-command, squinted up at the sky. "Aye. Even if this storm breaks, we've enough done to hold the foundation. Go track down the wee lassie, afore Ella has a conniption."

Nodding his thanks to the other men, Lachlan started across the yard. Likely Simone had gone down to the loch again to fish with the baker's son.

Although…

Suddenly frowning, Lachlan glanced up at the sky again. Dark clouds had started gathering about an hour ago, and if the storm hit while the lass was out on the water…

Bursting into motion, he ran toward his daughter's nursemaid, fear and panic not yet taking over, but the threat was there.

"Ella!" He crashed to a stop once he reached the woman, and took in a deep breath. "How long has she been gone?"

"Oh, milord!" the woman wailed, "ye ken I like a wee nap

some mornings, and she wasnae in the nursery when I awoke."

And why should she be stuck in a damn nursery all day?

Simone loved adventure as much as he did, and would've seen no good reason to be stuck in the nursery, with nothing more to do than watch an old woman nap.

Frowning, Lachlan glanced around the yard, as if his wee lass might easily be found there.

"Ye've looked for her?" She'd been missing for a few hours by his calculations, knowing how long Ella's naps usually took.

The woman was nodding her head and wringing her hands. "Aye! Aye, milord. I looked in the nursery and yer room and the great hall."

That was it?

Simone wouldn't be in any of those places, not when the great wide world beyond beckoned.

He did his best to stifle his sigh. It wasn't Ella's fault; he knew she was too old to be in charge of a wee hellion like Simone.

What the lass needs is a mother.

God's Wounds! Where in damnation did *that* thought come from?

When a clap of thunder sounded in the distance—the Almighty himself lending his opinion on the matter—Lachlan shook his head, focusing on his current concern.

"Find Martin and have him organize a search party. I'm going to check with the baker and the fishermen."

"A—aye, milord," Ella stuttered, as she offered an awkward curtsey.

But Lachlan was already hurrying past her, heading for the gates, and doing his best to ignore the ominous clap of thunder—which was much closer this time. He called out to his men as he began to jog, ensuring Martin would have plenty of help searching the keep for his missing daughter.

He didn't wait for the others, because he thought it might save them all a lot of time and stress if he found her quickly by searching the most likely places first.

But nearly an hour later, thoroughly drenched from the furious rain pouring down, Lachlan stood alone on the shores of his loch, his daughter nowhere to be found.

The baker hadn't seen her, nor had the baker's son, nor any of the fishermen. They'd predicted the weather would turn bad and few had ventured out onto the water that day. Those that did had all returned hours ago, and hadn't seen Simone then either.

But there was still one boat missing.

Lachlan's heart felt as if it would beat out of his chest, it hurt so much.

Saints above, protect her. Protect my angel.

God help him, but if Simone had been out there on the loch when this storm had hit, if she was now gone…

Nay, donae think it.

But how could he not?

"Nothing, milord!" called one of his men, holding a torch aloft as he jogged up from the path to the village.

Lachlan whirled. "Keep searching!" He bellowed. "All of ye! We *will* find her!"

A ragged chorus of "Aye, milords" rang up and down the shoreline.

God's Wounds, but it was damn near impossible to see the village, much less a wee lass out on the loch. "Someone head back to the keep and check with Martin."

He had to yell just to be heard over the crashing of the waves. The storm had begun to move on, with the thunder echoing in the distance, but the wind was still vicious.

A band tightened around his chest, refusing to allow him

to breathe properly. She was *out there*, he knew it! And if the waves had capsized her boat…

With a groan, Lachlan began to stalk down the shore, wishing for an enemy to slay or a demon to battle. This uncertainty, this fear, was the worst thing he'd ever experienced.

And as the rain lessened, he knew he wouldn't be able to hide the tears on his cheeks, and he didn't care.

But as the skies became a little clearer, he found he could see better too. He was far from the village—far from *anything,* but imposing cliffs. There was no place for a lost little girl to hide here.

But there, ahead of him on the shore…

Was that her boat?

Unconsciously, Lachlan let out a wordless bellow and began to run toward the beached lump.

Aye, aye, 'twas!

He wasn't sure if this fierce burning in his chest was hope, or fear, but he refused to allow himself to feel either.

The boat had been overturned, and the closer he came, the deeper the pit in his stomach became.

If the boat was here, overturned, on the beach, then that meant…

Not daring to breathe, not daring to pray, Lachlan reached the boat, and his heart in his throat, grabbed for the gunwale to flip it over. Mayhap there was a clue in there to where his daughter had gone overboard, where he could look for her.

He took a deep breath.

Dear God in Heaven, let her be safe.

CHAPTER 7

When the storm clouds had started closing in, Simone had just caught a fine, fat trout. She was laughing as she tried to remove the hook, while the poor thing flopped around on the bottom of the wee rowboat.

"Fine work," Mellie said, joining the girl in her laughter. "But that's our last fish for the day."

With a triumphant cry, Simone lifted her prize by the lip. "But 'tis bigger than both of yers! Ye're just going to let me win the wager?"

Mellie eyed the shore, then the clouds. "Aye, I think I must concede defeat. I still think Loch Ness is small, but ye're a better fisherwoman than I am."

Giggling, the lass nodded as she dropped her catch in the pail they'd brought along for just that reason. "Both of mine are winners, methinks. Cook will praise me—and ye too, I'll wager—when we have 'em for dinner tomorrow."

A distant crack of thunder startled Mellie, and she shifted around on the bench, settling into the rowing position.

Sainte Vierge!

She should've been paying better attention to the skies!

A piss-poor fisherman I turned out to be.

Simone glanced up from her catch to eye the sky as well. "Do ye think…" She swallowed, as if suddenly realizing the danger. "Do ye think we'll be caught in that storm?"

With a grunt, Mellie shipped the oars, settling them into their oarlocks. "No' if I can help it." She pulled hard on the starboard oar, turning their wee craft toward the Fraser shoreline. "But it might be close."

"I'm sorry, Mellie," Simone said in a small voice from her spot in the bow. Her grip was white-knuckled around the gunwale as she eyed the storm clouds above them. "I should've been paying attention."

Mellie's feet were braced against the opposite bench, her concentration on the task at hand. Still, she was pleased the girl was facing the shore and couldn't see the lightning strikes behind her.

Bon Dieu!

Had the storm really snuck up on them so suddenly?

Only a few moments ago, the skies had been clear. She *thought* they had been at least.

Was it possible she'd been enjoying herself so much with Simone, more time had passed than she'd realized?

With another grunt, Mellie pulled hard on both oars, welcoming the burn in her arms and back. "Just keep an eye on the shore, lassie, and tell me when we are close."

With a nod, Simone turned her attention back over Mellie's shoulders, and Mellie had to smile. The girl was adventurous, aye, as well as intelligent. 'Twas clear she'd been raised by a parent who cherished her, and Mellie knew Lachlan would never put the lass in the same position Mellie's father had put *her* in.

She'd agreed to this outing in the hopes of learning more about Lachlan, but had discovered she adored Simone's company because of the girl herself. The lass was witty and fun, full of silly faces and bad jokes. And her joy—at such simple pleasures—made Mellie happy as well.

I'll get her back safe.

But when the Heavens opened, Mellie began to doubt her vow.

The rain came down needle-sharp, and although Simone did her best not to complain, it became clear the lass was crying as she huddled under her plaid.

Mellie pulled on the oars for all she was worth, but the shore didn't seem to be any closer. The winds had whipped up waves bigger than she'd ever seen, and more than a few towered over their wee rowboat, threatening to capsize it.

"Simone!" she yelled, holding the girl's gaze even as she heaved on the oars. "Take off yer gown!"

"The water's freezing!" the lass shouted back, sobbing.

When she shook her head, Mellie's waterlogged braid barely moved. "Ye'll survive the cold, but if ye go overboard, the gown will drag ye down."

Nodding, the girl began to unlace her kirtle with shaking fingers, still crying in fear. That sight, more than anything, gave Mellie the strength to keep going.

She would not allow Lachlan's daughter to drown.

How long would this storm last?

Jagged lightning flashed so close nearby, Mellie could *taste* it.

It felt like hours by the time Simone removed her gown and huddled only in her leine, her wee lips blue from cold, and her chin jutting determinedly. Mellie thought her arms would pull from her sockets, but she bit her lip and kept pulling.

There was enough water in the bottom of their boat now to make her wish she could take a break to bail. But a glance over her shoulder told her she was making *some* headway against the waves, and she couldn't give up now.

It was Simone who dumped her bucket of fish over the side—which was a remarkable sacrifice for a six-year-old, Mellie thought in passing—and began to bail. Her teeth were chattering, but she looked just as determined as Mellie felt, and the woman called encouragement to the little girl as often as she could spare the breath.

Her fingers were cramped from her grip, and her palms splintered, when Simone glanced up.

"Mellie, look!" she cried, though her words were barely audible over a crash of thunder.

Mellie couldn't afford to look, but prayed she guessed correctly at what it was the girl wanted to show her.

Surely God wouldn't put more obstacles in their way now?

Leaning forward, she heaved one last time on the oars, and their boat made shore.

She almost cried out in joy.

Sainte Vierge! Blessed Mother of God, my thanks. Thank ye for Simone's life, and for mine!

Mother Mary knew how badly she wanted to rest, to slump over the oars and allow her back to recover.

But Simone needed shelter, so Mellie forced herself to turn...then gaped up at the cliffs towering above them.

There was no shelter there. And with the storm raging so brutally, even by the lightning flashes, she could see there was no shelter nearby.

"Is the village close?" Mellie asked her young companion, as she offered her hand to Simone to clamber over the benches.

The girl grabbed her sodden gown as she shook her head. "There's *naught* close," she hollered over the storm.

That's what I was afraid of.

Mellie could barely make her back work as she straightened, then all but rolled out of the boat into the surf.

Grabbing the gunwale, she shoved the boat further onto shore. At this point, it was their only shelter, as far as she could see, and she'd make use of it the best she could.

She pulled the oar from the lock, allowing it to fall into the water, and was pleased when Simone did the same for the other. Then the girl grabbed the opposite gunwale and began to heave along with Mellie.

Her strength was negligent, and her help minimal, but the knowledge the girl was fierce and determined made Mellie smile.

Despite the needle-sharp rain and the crashing waves, despite the lightning, which had them ducking every few seconds, they managed to get the boat out of the surf for the most part.

"Now what?" Simone shouted.

Instead of answering, Mellie pointed to the girl's side of the boat, hoping she'd understand the plan.

Mellie hiked up her skirt—glad now she'd changed into the simple gray gown she'd worn the day she'd followed Lachlan into the alleyways of Scone—and planted one knee on the gunwale. As the waterlogged rowboat began to tip, she leaned more weight on it and reached for the opposite side, which was lifting.

It was precarious and dangerous, and it caused her arms to ache even more. But when Simone began to push from her side, they managed to tip the boat up completely on its side.

A bit farther, and the entire boat toppled toward her.

She heard Simone cry out a warning, but it was too late. Besides, this had been Mellie's plan, even if she hadn't quite thought it through all the way.

The rowboat came crashing down atop her, one of the benches slamming against her shoulder and dazing her. Trapped under the boat, she was pushed into the sand. One hand was caught under the side of the boat, which sent pain shooting clear up her arm, and she wondered if she'd broken any fingers.

Sainte Vierge, let me rest!

But she couldn't. Simone was out there in the storm, and she needed Mellie.

With a curse, she pulled her fingers out from under the gunwale, and shifted to her hands and knees. Her shoulder ached fiercely, but she couldn't allow herself to focus on that at the moment. Instead, she planted her hands and straightened her arms, and began pressing back against the bench.

With another grunt from her, the boat lifted, but just slightly.

"Mellie!" came Simone's scream.

She wished she had the strength to answer, and prayed the girl would understand why she couldn't.

"Mellie!" came the cry again, and then—miracle of miracles!—a stone was shoved under the gunwale.

It allowed Mellie to rest, even if for only too brief a moment, by holding the boat off the ground on one side. Simone's frantic face appeared at the opening it made.

"Mellie, are ye aright?"

"Get in here, lass," Mellie managed to grind out past her clenched jaw.

Simone disappeared, but a moment later, another stone appeared. Then the girl offered a tight nod. "I'm ready."

With Mellie lifting and Simone wriggling, soon they were both under the boat, the stones propping it up and allowing Mellie to collapse, exhausted, in the wet sand.

They were safe, if not exactly warm and dry. The waves still lapped against the stern of the boat—and their feet—while the rain pounded above them. Lightning crashed and thunder boomed, but here, they wouldn't be harmed.

Thank ye, sainted Mother of God.

Simone whimpered and threw herself atop Mellie as well

as she could under the confines of the rowboat. Mellie wrapped her arms around the shivering, sobbing girl, and rolled to one side.

She curled herself around the lass, knowing, even wet, her body heat would help to keep her somewhat warm. She made sure the girl's head was pillowed on her shoulder—even though the pressure reminded her of her recent injury—and wrapped her other arm around her tiny body.

"Shh, honey. 'Twill be aright. We are safe here." A sudden thought made her stiffen. "Unless this loch has tides?"

Through her sniffles, Simone gave a weak sort of chuckle. "Nay, the water will nae—"

A loud burst of thunder overhead caused Simone to jump and cry out. When Mellie tightened her hold on the wee one, Simone eventually sighed and relaxed a bit.

Mellie herself was freezing, but Court had long ago taught her how to control her body's reaction to minor discomfort, and she used that mental trick now to make sure she didn't succumb to shivers.

It was a long time—impossible to tell how long—that they lay there in the wet sand, Mellie rubbing the girl's back and whispering calming words each time the thunder crashed overhead.

The rain ran under their makeshift shelter, creating little rivulets in the sand, and Mellie worried she should've had Simone garb herself again. But at least, with the quick-thinking lass's stones to prop up the gunwale, they had fresh air and a bit of light—however dim—in their shelter.

After a long time, that light began to grow a bit, and the thunder seemed to move farther away. It was only then that Mellie realized Simone was staring up at her.

"Are ye feeling better?" Mellie asked, pleased she didn't have to yell over the noise of the storm any longer.

But Simone didn't answer. Their noses were so close,

they were almost touching. She stared at Mellie with wide gray eyes, her freckles becoming visible as the afternoon lightened.

Was the girl in shock?

"Simone?" she prompted again, becoming worried.

She could turn over again, lift the boat and shove the girl out through the crack, but how hard would it be for Mellie herself to wriggle out?

And *Sainte Vierge,* was she in any shape to carry Simone all the way back to the village?

She *would* be, by God.

"Ye saved me," Simone finally whispered.

Mellie was so relieved the girl had spoken, she barely noted the words Simone had said.

Instead, she tightened her hold, until she was hugging the girl. "Aye, of course, honey. I cannae allow ye to come to harm, even for two prize fish."

The lassie's lips tugged into a frown. "I still won though. Even if I did lose the trout."

"Ye sacrificed them to save us." Mellie worked her arm free and tweaked the wee nose in front of her. " 'Twas a verra brave thing to do."

To her surprise, Simone flushed and looked away.

"What is it?" Mellie prompted gently. Her years with the Angels had taught her everyone reacted to near-death experiences in different ways. "Ye can tell me."

"I wish…" Simone tucked her head under Mellie's chin, so her next words were muffled. "I wish ye were my mother."

And God help her, but the girl's whisper wrapped around Mellie's heart and *squeezed,* until she had trouble breathing.

Simone was six years old.

The age her own bairn would've been.

Tears suddenly flooded Mellie's eyes, and she buried her face in the girl's wet hair, unsure what to say.

Had this farce of a betrothal been real, she might've been able to assure Simone she would make a good mother. Because in that moment, Mellie knew she *would* make a good stepmother. She'd waited years for the chance, never begrudging the work she did for the Queen, but always yearning for something more.

This…this *mission* to An Torr might've been her chance, had it been a real betrothal.

But it wasn't.

She was here with a job to do. She was an *Angel*.

And this precious wee lass in her arms had given her the opening she needed, if she could take it.

"I think…" God help her, could she question the girl, after everything they'd been through? She *had* to. She *had* to know if Lachlan was the good man he appeared to be, or the evil one she suspected. "I think yer mother would be verra proud of ye, and who ye've become."

From her spot under Mellie's chin, Simone snorted. "She wouldnae care. She left because she didnae love me enough."

Mellie stiffened. "Who told ye that?"

Was that what Lachlan had told his daughter?

"Ella." Simone pulled away enough to peek up at Mellie. "Only she didnae say it like that. But 'tis the truth."

"Nay," Mellie began, trying to reassure the girl. "I'm sure she loved ye verra much, but she had to…"

What lie would be convincing?

When Simone shook her head, she knocked against Mellie's bruise, releasing a hiss from Mellie the girl failed to notice. "Ye're wrong. I ken what happened. Mother didnae want to be married to Da, and she didnae want to be a mother to me, so she left us both." Her eyes pooled with tears. "If she'd loved me at all, she would've stayed."

Didnae want to be married…?

Even as Mellie wrapped the girl in her arms once more and murmured soothing words, her mind was churning.

Was it true?

Or was it more likely the lass had overheard something and guessed incorrectly?

Why would *any* woman not want to be married to a man as fine as Lachlan?

As fine as Lachlan.

Only this morning, she'd been questioning herself and her opinions of the Fraser laird. She'd wanted to learn the truth about him, to determine if he was as good a man as everyone believed. She'd thought if she could discover the truth of his past, she would know the truth of his loyalties.

If she knew the truth of his loyalties, she would have a better chance of succeeding in her *real* mission: determining if Lachlan was capable of masterminding a plot against the Crown.

And here she had it.

As fine a man as Lachlan.

If Simone was right—if he *hadn't* sent his former betrothed away—then mayhap he really *was* a fine man. A man who any clan would be proud to claim as their leader.

A good man.

A man who wasn't guilty of treason.

Sainte Vierge, but her mind was a mess. Her body ached, her fingers were cramped, and her shoulder throbbed. Even though they were now safe, her mind couldn't relax.

She had so many questions and—

Simone jerked. "Did ye hear that?"

Mellie had.

"Aye," she whispered.

The rain was slowing now, and somewhere in the distance, she'd heard a man's shout.

The girl pulled back to grin up at Mellie, her expression of hope warring with the tear marks on her cheeks.

"We're saved!"

Mellie allowed herself to exhale.

"Aye," she whispered again.

She held her breath, straining her ears to hear more. But other than the thunder fading in the north, they heard no more voices.

Which made the sudden shower of wet sand—as someone skidded to a stop on the other side of their makeshift shelter—a shock.

The two of them must've made some kind of noise, because the man cried, "*Simone? God in Heaven, Simone?*"

Lachlan!

His strong fingers curved under the gunwale, and he heaved with barely any exertion, wrenching the rowboat up off their rocks and exposing them to the now gentle rain.

But Mellie didn't care. She clutched his daughter and stared up at their savior, his shock mirroring her own expression, she was certain.

"*Mellie?*" he blurted in a ragged whisper.

And that's when she realized what he was asking.

All he could see was a bundle of wet wool and her hair. He didn't yet know his daughter was safe.

She forced herself to relax, to peel her arms away, so that the lass could peek up at her father.

"Da?" she choked.

With a wordless cry, Lachlan heaved the boat completely upright, rolling it off them as if it weighed nothing. The force showered them with sand, but no more than he did when he threw himself to his knees there beside them and reached for his daughter.

"Simone," he choked, pulling the girl from Mellie's arms and burrowing his nose in her hair. "My precious lassie."

Simone wrapped her own arms around her father, and when he began to rock back and forth, whispering harsh words of thanks to the Heavens against her hair, she patted his back.

"I'm aright, Da. Mellie saved me. She kept me safe."

Lachlan's eyes flashed open and he stilled, his daughter still crushed against his chest. He met Mellie's eyes, and she suddenly realized how ridiculous she must look.

Awkwardly, she pushed herself upright, smoothing her hair back from her forehead in a fruitless attempt to compose herself.

He was still staring at her.

She swallowed, and unbidden, her thumbnail rose to her lips. She *wanted* to look away, to try to calm the pounding in her heart, at least until she could make sense of her reaction to this man.

But she couldn't.

Instead, she watched as the terror in his eyes faded, to be replaced by something akin to wonder.

"Thank ye, Mellie," he whispered.

She shrugged uncomfortably. " 'Twas naught."

Simone placed her hand on her father's cheek and turned his head to look at her. " 'Twas *no'* naught, Da. She rowed us to shore in the storm. She flipped the boat. Her shoulder's bleeding."

Surprised, Mellie glanced down at her shoulder, and found she *was* bleeding, right where the bench had slammed into her. Through the rip in her kirtle and leine, the scrape was visible, and was already surrounded by a bruise. It was the sight of an old scar—something she'd rather Lachlan not see—which had her tugging at the material.

Simone had released her father, who had turned his incredulous gaze back to Mellie. "Ye truly are a wonderful mystery, milady."

"I could say the same about ye." The words burst from her lips before she could stop them.

Lachlan's own lips curled gently into a smile, as he settled his daughter against his shoulder. "Ye have only to ask, lass. I told ye I'd share all my secrets with ye. But for now..." He heaved himself to his feet, Simone's arms around his neck, and offered his hand to Mellie. "Let's get ye both home."

Home.

Thinking of the feel of the precious lass in her arms, and the words Simone had spoken, Mellie felt her throat close up with longing.

Could someplace like An Torr have been her home?

Could she have had a daughter like Simone?

Had things been different...

After only the briefest of hesitation, she placed her hand in Lachlan's, and couldn't hold back the groan as she pushed herself to her feet. She was here now, and although her mission was more confused than ever, she truly believed she'd been wrong about Lachlan.

He *was* a good man.

"Aye," she choked out. "Let's go home."

CHAPTER 8

Lachlan barely remembered the journey home.

His mind was a jumble of intense gratitude, awe, and lingering excitement. With his daughter against one shoulder, and his other arm around the most intriguing woman he'd ever met, he did his best to lead them back to the village.

He tried to imagine what it would've been like for the two of them, out on the loch alone, in such a violent storm. The Frasers had lost experienced fishermen in such storms before, but Mellie—a haughty *lady*—had not only rowed them to shore, but had also managed to create a shelter for her and Simone, and had kept his daughter safe.

He saw Mellie stumble often, and he kept eyeing the bruise forming on her shoulder. The bruise, and the old scar he'd seen beside it.

The scar which looked suspiciously like an arrow pock.

He decided that was a story for another time, if she'd even tell it, and pushed it to the back of his mind.

Thanks to the storm, the summer afternoon was chilly, and he could feel Simone shivering. And although Mellie stared stoically ahead, he could feel her shaking as well under his arm.

Because of the cold?

Or was she in shock?

Thankfully, Owen saw him coming and hollered to the other men. It was his commander himself who scooped Mellie up when she stumbled for the last time.

And although Lachlan had his hands full with Simone, a part of him felt a flash of irritation to see Mellie draped in his best friend's hold.

Why?

Was he...*jealous*?

Why no'?

She's my betrothed, is she no'?

After yesterday, after that aborted seduction, Lachlan would've said she was only here on the Queen's orders. Only here to test his loyalty.

But that was before she'd risked her life to save his daughter. Before he found Mellie carefully cradling Simone as if she cared a great deal for the lass.

Cupping the back of his daughter's head, he buried his face in her damp hair once more and inhaled gratefully, thanking God for sending Mellie to An Torr. Whatever reason she was here, Simone would be dead without her.

When they reached the keep, and his people realized what they were seeing, a gradual cheer rose. He *knew* they were all cheering for the safe return of his daughter, thinking he'd saved her, but soon enough, he'd set them straight on who Simone's savior really was.

For now though...

He took the stairs up to the top floor as quickly as he could, bellowing for a hot bath to be delivered to the nursery and Mellie's room, along with nourishing soup for both of them.

He skidded to a stop in the hall and turned to the lady's chambers, where Mellie was staying. "Brigit!" That was the maid's name, wasn't it?

The young woman pulled the door open, and he noticed she appeared as if she'd been crying. "Aye, milord? Ye've found Mellie?"

"I didnae even ken yer mistress was missing, lass." One more thing to address…later. With a dismissive sound, he jerked his head toward Owen, who was coming up the stairs carrying Mellie. "Warm her and help her bathe, Brigit, then make sure she eats her supper. She's likely exhausted."

Mellie made a weak noise, but he didn't stick around to listen to her protests. Instead, he shifted his hold on Simone and continued to the nursery, where Ella made a fuss over her "lost lamb."

With his hands clasped behind his back, Lachlan stood at the edge of the room and watched the bevy of servants fuss over Simone, bathing her and washing her hair, before sitting her in front of a roaring fire—warm enough to dry Lachlan's shirt and kilt in no time—and brushing out her hair as Ella spooned soup into her.

He felt damn near useless, but he couldn't make himself leave either. He kept his eyes locked on his daughter, as if she might disappear on him again, while intently eying her features and thanking the Almighty every other heartbeat.

She's safe. She's safe.

Tomorrow, he'd have a long talk with her about her safety, and probably create a dozen more of those rules she so despised, but he *would* keep her safe.

"Enough!" he finally barked, noticing Simone's eyelids grow heavy. "Out with ye!"

As the remaining maids curtsied and filed past, he made sure to thank each of them. More than one blushed at his praise and hurried out the door. Soon, only Ella remained.

Lachlan stepped forward to scoop his daughter off the floor, reveling in the feel of her, safe in his arms. "To bed with ye, lassie," he murmured, crossing the room.

As he tucked her in, she took hold of his hand. "I'm sorry, Da," she said in a small voice.

"Ach, dinnae fash," he said, as he placed a kiss on her forehead. "We'll make some new rules, but none of us kenned how quick that storm would come up. Ye're safe now."

Simone tugged at his hand until he sank down beside her on the bed. "Mellie really *did* save me, ye ken. She was so strong, and kenned exactly what to do."

He pictured the wee boat amid the storm-tossed waters, struggling to make headway toward the shore. He remembered the feel of Mellie's blistered hand in his, and the look of exhaustion on her face.

Had she been warmed yet?

Fed?

Was she sleeping now?

Suddenly, the urge to check on her was as overpowering as the need to watch over his daughter. He leaned down and placed another kiss on her nose.

"Sleep now, my precious. I'm going to go see to Mellie."

Simone's eyes were already closed.

"Love ye, Da," she whispered sleepily.

He squeezed her hand.

"And I love ye, more than ye'll ever ken," he whispered in return.

Turning, he nodded to Ella, a silent command not to let the lassie out of her sight. She must've understood, because she sank into a chair with a weary sigh, and not for the first time, Lachlan wondered about finding a new, younger nursemaid to keep up with his hellion of a daughter.

Or a wife.

Glancing once more at Simone, he saw she was fast

asleep, so he allowed himself to release her hand and stand. Leaving her was difficult, but there was something in him—some visceral urge—which told him he needed to see Mellie.

He needed to make sure she was safe as well.

When he reached her chamber, he knocked softly on the door, but received no response.

Was Brigit not sitting with her mistress?

Frowning, he pushed open the door, and was surprised to see the chamber dark. The hearth was cold—a fire hadn't even been laid—and the shutters were closed.

Where in damnation was that woman?

"Mellie?" he called in a low voice, wondering if he should go down to look for her in the great hall.

But a noise from the bed pulled him in that direction.

There was a mound under the coverlet, one Lachlan had thought was a pile of pillows. As he got closer, however, he could see the truth: it was Mellie, huddled on her side, with only the top of her head visible.

Lachlan dropped to one knee beside the bed.

"Mellie?" he inquired again, then pulled back the coverlet. Under that was another, and under that, a Fraser plaid, wrapped around the shoulders of...

God's Blood, she looked pitiful.

Mellie was huddled on her side, her shoulders tucked up around her ears, her arms wrapped around her knees, and she was shivering. Not the teeth-chattering kind of shiver, but the bone-deep shiver, where it feels as if you'll never get warm again.

Her eyes were closed.

He was moving, before he even realized his intentions.

His boots were easy enough to pull off, and his clothing had dried over the hour he'd stood in Simone's room. Doing his best not to jostle the bed too much, he pushed back the coverlets and crawled in beside her, taking her in his arms and throwing one thigh over her legs.

From the way she stiffened slightly, he knew she was awake, but she made no sound and still kept her eyes closed. It took a little wriggling, but he managed to get his right arm under the pillow, so her head was resting on his shoulder, and he was able to spread his hand across her back in order to give her as much of his heat as possible.

It took several long moments before he felt her relax, and even longer still until her shivering ceased. He ran his free hand up and down her arm, hoping to warm her further. The leg which was thrown over hers seemed to be putting off enough heat, but God Almighty, she felt so soft underneath him.

Her legs and hands were trapped under his thigh, and each soft little sigh she made tested his control. If she so much as twitched her fingers, she'd be able to feel how hard his cock was.

Squeezing his eyes shut, he thought of the fury of a summer storm. He thought of bathing in the frigid loch in the spring. He thought of his terror when he saw the overturned rowboat.

Not a single thing seemed to soften his desire.

God's Blood!

She was the most incredible, intriguing, *curious* woman he'd ever met. She'd rowed through a Highland storm to save his daughter, and had held a knife to a man's throat to save Lachlan himself. She'd gone down on her knees to try to get what she wanted from him.

She was sensual and gorgeous and strong and confusing as hell.

And she was here, in his arms, in a *bed*.

"Why are ye here?"

The whisper startled him. When he opened his eyes, he found her staring at him, their faces only inches apart.

"Ye were cold," he offered. "Why did Brigit abandon ye like this?"

She hadn't moved, and didn't so much as blink now. "I told her I was aright and ordered her to leave, over her protests."

"Are ye?"

"Once she left, I guess…" Finally her gaze shifted, locking on his chin, instead of his eyes. "I didnae realize how cold I actually was."

He rubbed at her arm again, the linen of her leine feeling entirely too thin under his touch. "Did ye eat? Did ye have a warm bath?"

She didn't respond, and her silence spoke volumes.

"Ah, lass." He gathered her close again, not even caring if she could feel the thickness of his cock pressed against her leg. "What ye did today…" He shook his head. "Ye leave me in awe."

"Because I rowed a boat?" Her voice was muffled against his chest.

He chuckled. "Because of yer strength and bravery. Did the healer, at least, see to ye?"

In response, she wriggled, putting some distance between them, so she could pull her hands out from under his thigh and straighten her legs. He loosened his hold, knowing they'd both be more comfortable that way.

"Here." She held up her hands, her palms bandaged with linen. "Brigit is more than capable, and I told her no' to bother the healer. The blisters will fade in a few days."

He pushed himself up on one elbow as he examined her dressings. Then, satisfied, he asked nonchalantly, "And yer shoulder?"

She'd rolled onto her back and unconsciously lifted one

wrapped hand to her right shoulder, where Simone had told him the boat's bench had come crashing down on her.

" 'Tis naught, as I said. A scrape was causing the wee bit of blood, and the bruising will go down. I've had worse."

The last part slipped out, judging from her slight wince, so he knew she hadn't meant to tell him that.

Knife-wielding, seduction, rowboat-flipper, and now Lachlan could add "combat injured" to her list of accomplishments.

Since she'd given him the opening, he decided to press her.

"Like an arrow wound?"

Before she could deny it, he leaned over her and brushed her hand out of the way, so he could touch her right shoulder himself.

"I saw it through the rip in yer kirtle." He could feel the bandage under her leine, and was pleased Brigit had cared for her mistress's wounds at least.

Her eyes flicked toward his, then fixed on the bed curtain above them. He could *see* her mind furiously whirling.

Was she trying to come up with some lie to explain the old wound?

"Mellie?"

She swallowed. " 'Twasnae life-threatening. Just a graze."

A graze with an *arrow* wasn't to be dismissed. And it wasn't the sort of mark he thought he'd find on his betrothed.

"Who *are* ye, Mellie?" he whispered.

She stiffened for a moment, then relaxed into a languid smile, as she rolled onto her side to face him.

"Who do ye want me to be?" she asked in a husky voice, as she lifted her hand to his cheek.

But he intercepted it, holding her gently, so as not to hurt her palms any further. All he knew was, after the progress they'd made—and they *must* be making progress, because he was far more confused than he'd been when she'd arrived—he couldn't stand to have her touch him like that again.

Like a practiced seductress. Like someone who was used to changing herself to suit others.

Who do ye want me to be?

He met her eyes and willed her to understand. "Yerself, Mellie." Slowly, he drew her hand to his lips and kissed two of her fingertips. "I want ye to be yerself around me. Because ye can."

Something flashed in her blue eyes—worry?—and she tried to pull away. He kissed a third fingertip and noted her shudder as she dropped her gaze to his lips.

"Who are ye, Mellie?" he whispered, willing her to tell him the truth.

But instead of answering him, she yanked hard on her hand, clutching it to her chest, as she fell back against the pillow and glared up at him.

"Who are *ye*, Lachlan Fraser?" she shot back.

He blinked in surprise.

He'd never hidden any part of himself from her, had he?

"What do ye wish to ken?"

⁓

*E*verything.

Yesterday—*Sainte Vierge*, had it only been yesterday her seduction had failed so spectacularly?—he'd told her he'd always speak the truth to her.

Could she trust him?

Aye, she could.

She wanted to know *everything* about him, but couldn't ask it, not lying here in a strange bed, staring up at him as he loomed over her on one elbow. She had to narrow her questions to what mattered.

His loyalty to the throne?

That was why she was here, was it not?

The reason for this farce of a betrothal, the reason for her heartache and confusion and longing. She needed to discover if he was behind the assassination attempt.

What is it ye wish to ken?

"What happened to Simone's mother?"

As soon as she'd blurted the words, she gasped, lifting one bandaged hand to her lips.

Bon Dieu, what had she done?

Lachlan, for his part, only looked slightly startled. Recovering far more quickly than she, he shrugged.

"I'm surprised ye donae ken already. From what I've heard, that maid of yers likes to gossip."

How to take back her words?

"I shouldnae have—"

"Nay, 'tis aright." He offered her a smile—how had she never noticed how handsome he was when he smiled?—and settled his head on his palm once more.

When he rested his heavy hand against her belly, she realized he was preparing to tell her what she wanted to know.

She also realized she was suddenly very, very warm.

"I met Alice Stewart at the Bruce's court. She was beautiful and refined and haughty. Every man there lusted after her, but my father convinced her da I'd make a sound husband. The betrothal contract was signed, and she came to An Torr."

She counted in her head. "This would've been...seven years ago?"

"Aye." His thumb began to draw little circles on the linen covering her belly. "Da was still alive then, of course. She, ah..." He huffed slightly, and she wondered if it was supposed to be a chuckle. "She and I saw no reason to wait for the vows. She was nae virgin, mind ye, and we had our fun together, since we were to be married soon enough anyway. Or so I thought."

When he trailed off, she shifted under his hand. It felt so damn *good* to be lying here in bed with him, but she also needed to know more. "She became pregnant?"

"Aye." When one side of his lips pulled up, it wasn't quite a smile. "I was thrilled. She wasnae the kind of wife I would've picked, I'd come to realize, but a bairn…" This time his smile became genuine. "I'd always wanted to be a da, ye ken."

"I didnae," she whispered, transfixed by his smile.

"Aye, well…" His grin fell, and he shook his head, his gaze focusing on his hand where it rested on her belly. "When Simone was born, Alice told me she had no need for a girl child. A daughter couldnae become laird, couldnae cement her status."

A sour taste settled in the back of Mellie's throat as she realized Simone's tale from this afternoon had been *right*. The lassie's mother had left because she hadn't loved Simone enough.

"That's…" She shook her head, unable to understand a mother who would abandon her child. One who didn't realize how lucky she was to *have* one.

Still not meeting her eyes, Lachlan lifted one shoulder in a sort of shrug. "My father died soon after, and Hamish became laird. I think Alice and her father had concocted some sort of scheme to make *me* laird, assuming I would have an heir. When she realized it wouldnae work, when she realized I wouldnae be laird, she went back to her family." His voice dropped to a whisper. "She didnae even bother to wean the bairn. I had to scramble to find a wetnurse, and Hamish…" He shook his head.

"He disapproved?"

Finally, Lachlan looked up and caught her gaze. "He agreed with Alice. Said I was stupid to pine over a mere daughter, and stupid to let Alice go. But our broken betrothal didnae harm her, and she's married to some poor bastard out in the Western Isles."

Mellie shook her head. "And to think if she'd waited a few years, she would've gotten what she wanted; to be the wife of a laird."

"Nay, she wanted to be the wife of a laird right away, and she got that with her husband. And I…" Slowly, the hand on her belly began to move with gentle caresses. "I realized I didnae want Alice. I didnae want a haughty, cold noblewoman. I want a strong woman, a caring one. A woman I can trust."

Overwhelmed by the emotion she saw in his gray eyes and the sensations his touch was sending through her, Mellie shut her eyes.

A woman he could trust?

Sainte Vierge, help me.

He couldn't trust her, but she was coming to trust him.

Lachlan hadn't broken his first betrothal because Alice had given him a daughter. He loved Simone then, just as much as he did now.

He wasn't the villain.

Nay, Lachlan Fraser was a good man.

He was a *good man!*

Why did that certainty fill her with such a surge of joy?

A smile—one she couldn't have hid if she tried—curved her lips upward as she reached once more for him.

This time he didn't stop her, not when she cupped the back of his neck and drew him down toward her. He allowed her to brush her lips across his, but then he pulled back.

His eyes were darting between hers, as if looking for a lie.

"Ye're sure?" he whispered.

"Aye," she breathed in return, willing him to see her certainty. "I want this."

A woman I can trust.

Could Mellie, one day, be that woman?

Lachlan studied her, and she held her breath, even as she nodded slowly.

"The truth, Lachlan," she whispered.

She saw the exact moment he stopped fighting, stopped denying them both. With a groan of surrender, he lowered his head once more, his lips unerringly finding hers.

And this kiss—?

This kiss was *nothing* like what they'd shared yesterday, in his chambers.

Because this kiss was the *truth.*

But, just as he did the day before, he was the one to pull away, though this time he did so with a reluctant groan. Bracing his weight on one arm, he rested his forehead against the pillow beside her head, breathing heavily.

She could feel his hardness pressed against her thigh. A fortnight ago—yesterday, even!—she would've crowed with victory at this evidence of her success.

But now…?

Now she wasn't sure.

For the first time in her life, she was well and truly aroused by a man. Her body reacted to Lachlan in a way she'd never experienced before.

Oh, she'd felt arousal before, certainly, but never from just a kiss. Never from just the way a man sounded as he breathed near her.

"Mellie."

Never from the way a man groaned her name so helplessly.

Intrigued, she squirmed, and the contact of his hardness at the juncture of her thighs caused them both to gasp.

"Mellie," he repeated, more sharply, as he pushed himself upright. "I'll no' take ye like this."

She wasn't exactly sure she'd been offering, but she blurted the first thing which came to her mind. "I'm no' a virgin."

"Neither am I," he said with a shrug. "It matters naught. I'll no' have our first time together be…"

When he trailed off, Mellie realized she was holding her breath.

First time. He meant to have her.

Nay.

With Lachlan, 'twould be *making love.*

And that *would* be a first for her.

"I want ye, Mellie," he growled as he arched his back, pushing his member against her in a crude, *wonderful* reminder. "I've wanted ye since I first saw ye, but now?" He shook his head. "I'm in awe of ye, and confused as hell, and I *still* want ye so much, I'm afraid I'll spill if ye so much as grin at me."

Sainte Vierge, really?

Slowly, unintentionally, Mellie felt her lips curl upward.

Lachlan frowned.

"I mean it," he said sternly, then rolled off her.

She felt a moment of loss, before he settled onto his knees beside her on the bed. When he pushed back the coverlets, she shivered, but not because of the cold.

"Lift yer knees," he commanded.

Mellie was used to men giving her commands, but this? "What?"

Lachlan lowered his head until he was resting his weight on one planted fist, his nose inches from hers. "Lift. Yer. Knees."

His growled command, his intense stare, his *scent* all

bombarded Mellie's senses, until she could do naught more than scramble to lift her knees as he'd ordered.

"What—what are ye doing?" she managed to stammer, as he pushed himself upright.

His wicked grin reached down between her thighs and caused her muscles to clench so suddenly, she gasped.

He placed a hand on each knee. "Seducing *ye*."

It was the promise in his voice which had her arching her back, not bothering to contain her moan.

Sainte Vierge!

For the first time, Mellie wasn't in command of the seduction.

"Lachlan," she whispered.

"Look at me, lass," he commanded, and when she did, he nodded. "This isnae about my pleasure, do ye understand? Ye shouldnae look away."

What was he—?

And then he began inching her leine up, and she stopped thinking altogether.

"So beautiful," he murmured, wrapping one large hand around her ankle. His gaze was locked on her calf, his eyes caressing her, as his thumb made little circles on her skin. "Ye like it when I touch ye, do ye no? I can feel the way yer pulse jumps, right here."

And then he lifted her foot to his lips and brushed a kiss against the sensitive spot of her ankle, just below the little bump of the joint.

Sucking in a breath, she pushed herself up on her elbows.

His wicked grin turned her way once more. "Ye like that, lass?"

Mutely, she nodded.

"What *else* do ye like?" Holding her gaze—and her foot— he dragged his rough palm up her leg, until his fingertips rested against the inside of her knee. "Would ye like me to kiss ye *here?*"

There was an intensity in his gaze which told her he wasn't just teasing her.

She nodded again.

"Say it," he commanded. "Take control of yer pleasure, lass."

By all the saints, aye!

Desire pooled between her legs in a sort of liquid heat she welcomed. Her elbows took most of her weight as she lifted her hips just slightly, as if the center of her pleasure was reaching for him, and she had no control over it.

And it was all because of his *words*.

"Aye," she whispered harshly.

His hand didn't move. "Aye, what, lass?"

She cleared her throat and dropped her head back, so she was staring upward.

Was it easier to say if she wasn't looking at him?

"Aye. Kiss me there."

Before the words were out of her mouth, his lips were already brushing against the sensitive skin on the inside of her knee.

First one, then the other.

He was bent almost double, but when he planted one hand between her legs, and used the other to caress the outside of her thigh, she stopped caring about logistics.

"And now, Mellie?" he growled. "What do ye want me to do? Kiss yer neck? Fondle those sweet tits of yers?"

The vibrations of his voice reached down deep her in her center and shook her until she was near breathless.

"Nay," she managed to choke out.

"Tell me," he commanded again.

She squeezed her eyes shut. "Nay, I don' want ye to fondle my tits." She knew they were large, and most of her lovers had been focused on them as the main source of their pleasure.

But today wasn't about her past.

Lachlan had said this was about *her* pleasure.

So she accepted his challenge. She opened her eyes, lifted her head, and met his gaze. "I want ye to touch me."

Slowly, one of his brows rose in challenge. "How?"

Mellie couldn't back down now. She allowed herself to flop back on the pillows, reaching between them to ruck up her leine. The cooler air caressed her thighs, then her mount of curls, but she wasn't at all chilled.

Nay, it was the fire in his gaze—which she held in challenge—which warmed her.

"Donae let me dictate what ye like, lass. Tonight is for *ye*. Ye'll have to tell me what brings ye pleasure."

Did he think to embarrass her?

Did he think she would demur?

Nay, she knew what she liked, and despite the bandages on her palms, she would show him.

When she touched two fingers to her opening, he lost their silent battle and dropped his gaze to her wet slit. A slight grin lifted one side of her lips.

"Like this," she whispered.

It was the sight of those large hands reaching for her, hesitating slightly, then covering her fingers, which made her moan with pleasure and drop her head back on the pillow.

The man knew what he was doing, that was for certain.

He dragged the pad of one large thumb across her sensitive folds, then circled her pearl.

But mayhap she was different from other women, because that touch wasn't what made her go wild. Men had tried it before, and it was likely why she rarely found release during sex.

It was—

And then he slid a finger inside of her, and she stopped wondering what was wrong with her, because *Sainte Vierge* it felt good!

He'd leaned forward, the stubble of his cheeks caressing her sensitive inner thigh, and she suddenly *knew* what she needed.

"Kiss me," she gasped. Her hips bucked toward him as she repeated the command. "Kiss me!"

"Oh, thank the saints," he groaned, as his head bent forward.

It was the reverence in his voice, more so than even the sensation of his tongue on her most intimate parts, which sent Mellie teetering on the edge. She sucked in a gasp, wondering if she was really about to find fulfillment so quickly.

No man had ever done this for her. No man had ever cared so much about *her* pleasure. No man had ever cared for her at all.

It was the knowledge this man *did* care, and had made tonight all about her, which brought her so close to her release. God help her, but she was about to fall.

In more ways than one.

And then he dragged his other hand down her thigh to cup her arse. His fingers brushed against her second opening, the taboo one, and she bucked against his mouth, her release bursting upon her so suddenly, she cried out.

The waves of pleasure rolled over her as she flexed so hard, her hips came off the bed. He pressed his fingers into her, and she could swear he was smiling against her skin.

As she came back to earth, she sagged against the mattress, feeling boneless, and wondering if she should be embarrassed.

But he slid his fingers out of her and sat up, then pulled

her leine down, as if naught was wrong, then moved up to lie beside her.

Her heart was hammering inside her chest, torn between confusion and joy and exhaustion. Her back and shoulders ached, her palms burned, and she felt close to tears at any moment.

But he'd brought her pleasure.

On purpose.

A man had set out to bring her pleasure, without regards to his own, and had asked *her* for guidance on how to do it.

He'd given her control—

Nay.

Nay, she'd *taken* it.

When Lachlan wrapped his arms around her again, bringing her against his chest and cradling her as if she was special to him, Mellie almost lost her fight against her tears.

This man, this *good man*, treated her as if she was a prize.

And she was *betrothed* to him!

She ought to be joyful. She ought to be smiling, full of hope for their future together, where she'd become the lady of An Torr and Simone's mother.

But she couldn't.

Because no matter how good this man was, no matter how guilty or innocent he was of treason, she had to betray him.

Soon.

CHAPTER 9

Why in damnation did his betrothed have an *arrow wound* in her shoulder?

Was she really who she said she was?

Her stories about her childhood—shared over the last sennight, and a few since that horrible, wonderful evening in her arms—seemed real enough. Mayhap it wasn't *who* she was he was questioning…but *what*.

Mayhap she wasn't his betrothed at all.

Mayhap the Queen had sent her here for another reason.

With a growl, Lachlan slumped in his chair, frustrated by all the damnable *papers* which seemed to accompany being a laird. Father had always seemed to handle this with grace… or mayhap he'd just turned it all over to Martin and Gillepatric.

Stealing a glance out the open window, Lachlan stifled a sigh. He wanted to be out there now, training with his men or out on the loch.

Or with Mellie.

The idea gave him pause, and a slow smile tugged his lips upward. It'd been three days since that storm, since she'd saved Simone, and since she'd come apart in his arms. Sometimes he thought he could close his eyes and remember the taste of her on his tongue.

Those times necessitating him taking himself in hand, or he'd never been able to concentrate.

But as she'd been recovering in her room, she seemed... more relaxed. Twice now, Lachlan had stopped by to see her, and had been rewarded by the absolutely perfect sight of his daughter sitting cross-legged on Mellie's bed, the two of them giggling over something.

Once, Simone had been teaching Mellie some sort of string-game, and their voices melding in song had caused him to suck in an awed breath, before he'd even reached the room.

He and his daughter had dined in Mellie's room each evening—easier now that Mother and Gillepatric were gone—and those meals had been joyous each time.

When had there ever been this much laughter at An Torr?

It was wonderful, aye, but why did Lachlan get the feeling she was holding a part of herself back, somehow?

Who *was* she?

"Well, it looks as if ye've finally wet yer wick!"

Lachlan's gaze jerked up to see Owen lounging against the doorframe.

"What makes ye say that?"

"Because in the time I've stood here watching, ye've gone from smiling to satisfied to confused, and back again." The other man sauntered into the room and leaned a hip against the desk, as he crossed his arms with a smile. "Only a man who's finally tupped the woman he loves looks like *that*."

Lachlan scowled at his best friend's nonchalance. "*Any* man who can't figure a woman out looks like that."

Owen burst into laughter. "I retract my previous assumption. She's got ye wrapped in circles, aye? So ye havenae tupped her?"

"God's Wounds," Lachlan muttered, leaning back over the contracts on his desk and wondering if there was anything there to distract him from his friend's teasing. " 'Tis none of yer concern."

" 'Twas as I thought. Ye havenae." Owen chuckled in satisfaction, as he shifted his position, so his arse was all but planted on the desk. "When will ye?"

"Why are ye here?" Lachlan snapped out, jerking his gaze up to glare at his best friend.

Owen merely grinned. "Because I've missed teasing ye, what with ye hiding with yer love for the last few days. I've heard she's recovered?"

The reminder of that frantic search distracted Lachlan from his irritation, and the tension in his shoulders eased. "Aye. Simone has all but forgotten the ordeal, and Mellie is…" He shook his head in bemusement. "She is strong."

Strong.

The word hung between them, as the two men contemplated the mysterious woman in silence. Owen shifted again, and when Lachlan looked up, his friend was smiling once more.

"Ye love her, don' ye?"

Did he?

Lachlan's lips tugged down. He'd once thought he'd loved Alice, and look where that had gotten him. But Mellie…

He shook his head again. "She is beautiful and strong, aye. And intelligent. And she loves Simone, or at least she seems to."

But she was keeping a secret. He was *certain*.

"Ye're a lucky man, to love yer betrothed," Owen offered in a low voice.

But Lachlan sighed. "I don' love her. I barely ken her."

"I needed nae more than a glance to fall in love with my Mary."

Lachlan pushed away from his desk and propped his feet up with a scowl. "Ye met yer Mary when ye were drunk off yer arse at the Games, as I recall."

"Aye," Owen agreed, cheerfully, "but I tell her it was her wit which made my head spin so. And her beauty which had me stumbling so often."

Reluctantly, Lachlan felt a smile tugging at his lips, despite his intention to be annoyed by his friend's merriment. "And yer vomiting? Did ye tell her it was on account of her glorious singing voice?"

Owen nodded somberly. "Love can do odd things to a man's stomach, Lachlan."

Chuckling now, Lachlan made a rude gesture to his friend. "Ye're a buffoon sometimes. Why are ye *really* here, other than to try to convince me I love my betrothed?"

"Convince ye? Nay, I just wanted to plant the idea in yer head. Mary said if I didnae, she'd make *me* get up with the bairn tonight." Before Lachlan could do more than roll his eyes, Owen reached into the pouch at his belt. "Also, a messenger from Scone delivered this earlier, and I told Martin I'd deliver it."

With a crash, Lachlan's boots hit the floor, and he leaned forward to snatch the rolled parchment from his friend's hand. "Ye couldnae have *led* with this?"

Owen shrugged. "And miss teasing ye?"

But Lachlan wasn't paying attention. The scroll in his hands was small, and addressed to *Mellie*, and tied with a ribbon.

For a moment, he considered opening and reading it. He had questions about her identity and her reason for being at An Torr, and it was possible this letter may answer them all.

But she was his betrothed.

More than that, she was the woman he was suspecting Owen might be right about. He might very well be falling in love with Mellie Lamond.

"Go away," he commanded in a low voice.

"Say again?" Owen asked, in an overly cheerful tone.

Lachlan looked up, glaring. "Go away. Go make yerself useful and find Mellie."

"Find me for what?"

When Mellie stepped through the open doorway, both men rose to their feet, although Lachlan felt like an eager lad as he scrambled upright. He held the scroll out in front of him, as if it was a shield.

Mayhap it *was*.

She looked so lovely today—wearing that red gown again—and the sight of her lips reminded him of a particularly lurid fantasy he'd entertained last night. Aye, mayhap the letter was hiding the way his cock jumped.

Thankfully, Mellie hadn't appeared to notice.

"Do ye need me?" she asked again.

Offering a little bow, Owen smiled at her. "*Need* ye, gentle lady? My laird is positively desperate for ye."

"Go away, Owen," Lachlan growled.

His best friend sent a little smirk his way, before waving to them both on his way out the door. When Mellie turned back to the desk, one brow raised in question, Lachlan thrust out the scroll.

"Here," he blurted. "This came for ye."

Was it his imagination, or did she hesitate before she stepped forward?

"Ye didnae open it?"

When she reached for the letter, Lachlan's fingers instinctively closed around it, forcing her to tug and meet his gaze.

"Should I have?" he asked in a low voice.

She swallowed, and he was distracted by the slight flush which rose up her cheeks.

"Nay. 'Tis likely only news from the royal court. May I?"

Her answer was somehow too *perfect*.

He released the letter and watched as she opened and scanned it. It shouldn't surprise him someone as intelligent as Mellie could read, but he *was* surprised by the surge of pride he felt when he realized his wife would be so accomplished.

If she *did* become his wife.

As she read, one of her hands crept upward, until her fingernail was lodged firmly between her teeth. It was an odd, endearing little habit he'd noticed when she was uncomfortable.

What was she uneasy about now?

But despite her nail-biting, she lifted her gaze to his with a tight smile and passed the letter to him. "See? Naught but gossip from a good friend."

With a carefully neutral expression, Lachlan took the letter and read it.

My dearest friend,

We miss you here at Scone, but trust you are well. Without any word from you yet, we of course assume the worst, despite knowing you are likely safe. We ladies have so many faults, do we not? Perhaps the worst is our tendency to worry over those angels in our lives.

Courtney and Ross have returned safe, their journey successful. Ross has decided to remain here, as I believe the two of them have reached an understanding. I know you will join me in rolling your eyes at how long it took them to realize their love.

Our dear Charlotte has been delivered of a baby boy, only a *few days after Courtney's return. You will note, of course, that my counting calculations were correct. Her Majesty insisted on being present, and the two princesses have left off cooing over Alex, to fuss over wee Roger. The bairn is as fierce a warrior as his father, and is blessed with his mother's looks. We hope to <u>see you soon</u>, so you can meet him.*

I have more news to share, but it can wait until warmer times.

Anxiously awaiting news of An Torr.
Your very closest friend,
Lady Rosalind

Lachlan was frowning by the time he finished reading, then went back and re-read it. Such a simple missive, but the parchment it was printed on was longer, as if this Rosalind had intended to write more, but had run out of things to say.

What had she meant, when referring to warmer times?

It was high summer already; how much warmer did she expect it to get?

The point of the letter seemed to just be giving Mellie grief for not writing sooner. Well, that could be arranged.

He handed the letter back across the desk. "Would ye like some parchment to reply?"

"Thank ye," she replied, in a strangely subdued voice and avoiding looking at him as she rolled her friend's letter, "but I brought my own."

"The Ross in the letter. Fraser? My friend, who used to guard the Queen?"

Mellie's gaze flicked up to meet his just briefly, then away as she stepped backward. "A—aye. Mayhap 'twas why ye did no' see him afore we left for An Torr?"

"Where did he go with this Courtney?" The letter had

been vague on that point, clearly referencing something Mellie already knew. "What was the point of their journey?"

"I donae ken, milord," she said, almost to the door. "If ye don' mind, I'd like to re-read it afore composing my reply?"

Why in damnation was she acting so nervous around him?

He nodded gruffly, his thoughts on the letter. "Aye. And I'll have a messenger deliver it, if ye'd like?"

"Mayhap." She offered him a curtsey, which appeared nervous and far too formal. "Excuse me, milord," she said, then darted out of the room.

Lachlan sank back into his chair.

By all the saints in Heaven!

What just happened?

~

As Mellie hurried to the chambers she'd been given, she clutched Rosa's letter in her fist. It was only when she reached her door, she realized she'd crushed the poor parchment in order to control the shaking of her hand.

Damnation. That willnae be good for the message.

Not the message Lachlan just read. The *other* one.

Because as innocuous as Rosa's letter appeared, Mellie couldn't escape what her friend was actually telling her: *Report.*

The comment about worrying over an angel was a clear rebuke for not sending her report sooner. Rosa—especially now that Charlotte was abed—was likely going near-mad with concern over what Mellie had found at An Torr.

Trying to force herself to breathe normally, she darted into her room and stepped over to the open window.

Bon Dieu, why had this letter affected her so deeply?

Because she wasn't sure how to respond.

Could she respond?

Or did she need to return to Scone, to explain her feelings and failings?

"Milady?"

Mellie turned to see Brigit pushing the door closed behind her.

The younger woman seemed unusually serious. "Ye've had word from Scone? May I read yer letter?"

Frowning slightly, Mellie held the parchment out, pleased her hands were no longer shaking.

Brigit could read?

There was apparently quite a lot about her new maid Mellie didn't know.

Brigit's lips moved as she read, and when she was finished, she looked up with a grin. "Saints be praised Lady Charlotte is well! And Court and Ross have finally discovered their feelings for one another!"

Despite her intentions to remain focused, Mellie's brow went up.

Not only did her maid read, but she knew about Court and Ross's pasts?

Well, Brigit *was* excellent at collecting gossip, was she not?

"Aye," Mellie finally agreed, carefully choosing her words. "I believe Ross wasn't considered an ideal mate previously, but if he's been accepted as the Queen's guard once again, he must have passed Court's test."

It was a delicate way of hinting that Ross Fraser had been a prime suspect in the Queen's assassination attempt.

As was his former laird, Lachlan.

Her maid hummed thoughtfully, then handed the parchment back to Mellie. "So ye'll be needing yer writing implements, milady? To respond?"

She did, but first…

Holding the letter in front of her, Mellie lifted her other hand to her lips and chewed on a nail.

There was more to the letter, she was *sure* of it.

More news to share, but it can wait until warmer times.

Warmer times.

It was Rosa's way of hinting at how to reveal her secret message, the one she didn't want falling into Fraser hands.

When Brigit leaned over her shoulder, Mellie started and whirled. Her maid was looking down at the parchment, particularly the empty space at the bottom, and clucked her tongue.

"Lady Rosalind must've kenned ye wouldnae have easy access to oak galls."

It was so similar to Mellie's line of thought, she jerked her head up, piercing her maid with a suspicious stare. "*What?*"

Brigit reached over Mellie's arm and tapped the empty space with her fingernail. "Oak galls, to activate the vitriol. I ken Lady Rosalind is brilliant, but even she couldnae expect ye to have it on hand here in An Torr."

Mellie could only blink incredulously.

The younger woman was correct; one of Rosa's favorite ways of sending secret messages was to dissolve vitriol in water and write using that clear formula. The receiver could soak a sponge in water and oak galls, wipe it over the message, and create a primitive sort of ink.

But here at An Torr, Mellie couldn't just *ask* for oak galls, not without raising suspicion, and Rosa would've known that. Which left—

"Milk," Brigit said, then glanced up at Mellie and nodded knowingly. "I'll get a candle. 'Tis what she meant by warmer times, aye?"

Mellie could do little more than nod mutely.

Sainte Vierge!

Just who *was* this little maid of hers?

Brigit scurried back over, a hand cupped around the lit taper in her hand. Carefully, she placed it on the table, then stepped back, looking between it and the parchment in Mellie's hand with excitement.

Mellie's stomach knotted with more indecision.

The younger woman was right again; Rosa had likely written her message in raw milk, which, when activated by a hot flame, charred a darker shade and allowed the words to be read. It was a simple method, but almost foolproof.

Apparently, even palace maids knew of it.

Mellie lifted her chin, and said imperiously, "Ye are dismissed, Brigit."

But rather than be offended, the younger woman nodded cheekily. "I'll give ye a few minutes privacy. Better burn it when ye're done," she offered on her way out, as if Mellie wouldn't have done that anyhow.

How in the name of all the saints did *Brigit* know so much of the ways of the Queen's Angels?

Mellie shook her head, dismissing her questions as unanswerable as soon as the door closed behind Brigit.

She had work to do.

With shaking hands, she held the parchment near the flame, terrified of getting too close. She took a deep breath, forcing herself to remain calm, then tried again.

The trick was to focus on one patch of the parchment at a time, holding it above, but not too close to the heat. Slowly, the flame revealed letters, then full words began to emerge.

e + R killed RH leader—Andrew <u>Fraser</u>.
Says Fs are behind attempt, still supporting the Comyns for crown.
L is <u>guilty</u>.
Get out of there.

. . .

Mellie had to swallow down the bile, which threatened to creep up her throat, and force herself to focus on her task. The letter written in invisible ink—now revealed—would damn her as a spy at An Torr.

She couldn't allow herself to react to her friend's report until the evidence was destroyed. The flames licked too close to the parchment, and she allowed it, waiting for one corner to catch and spread.

Only when she had to drop it to the table to finish burning, only when the whole horrible letter had been consumed and turned to ash, only when she brushed those ashes out the window...only *then* did she allow herself to sink into the window seat and process what Rosa had written.

Court and Ross killed the Red Hand leader.

Andrew Fraser?

Lachlan's uncle—the one who'd disappeared so long ago, when he'd gone searching for his youngest nephew—had been named Andrew. But no one at An Torr had heard from him in years, according to Brigit's gossip, and what Lachlan had said that first night.

How could the Frasers be behind the assassination—according to Rosa—if Lachlan had no contact with that uncle?

Or was Lachlan just a very, very good liar?

Nay! He's a good man!

And a good man would not collaborate with traitors.

He *was not* guilty, no matter what Rosa and the Angels believed.

And there was no way she could explain that in a report.

"Are ye done yet?"

Mellie jumped and twisted toward the door. Brigit's head poked around the frame, a cheeky grin in place. As she saw her mistress scowling at her, she straightened and stepped into the room, holding a small jug.

"I thought ye might like to reply in kind." She held up the jug and waggled it as she crossed the room. "So I popped down to the kitchens and told them ye had a hankering for milk."

Bon Dieu, just who *was* this maid of hers?

Mellie shook her head, knowing the mystery of Brigit's sudden understanding of espionage would have to wait.

One problem at a time.

"I'll no' be replying."

Brigit stopped short, her brows nearly flying to her hairline. "No'? I can find a messenger for ye, if secrecy's what concerns ye. 'Tis why I was sent along with ye, after all."

Sent along?

Mellie shook her head. "I cannae reply by letter. I'm going back to Scone to report in person. Ye'll have to follow later with the luggage."

The little maid placed the jug on the table, one hand on her hip, and cocked her head as she studied Mellie. "*Why?* What do ye need to say, which cannae be said in a letter?"

Mellie lifted her chin, sure she was doing the right thing, but also unwilling to share too much of her mission with the maid, no matter how much the younger woman seemed to know. "The Queen believes certain things about Lachlan. I must answer those suspicions."

"Ye think he is a good man?"

The maid's question, so close to Mellie's own thoughts, was a surprise. Instinctively, she nodded. "I do."

The younger woman pursed her lips. "I don' pretend to ken yer history, or why ye were sent here, and I didnae ken ye well at court, but even *I* can see how happy ye are. How happy ye are with him. Ye'd give that up—give up yer happiness—for the Queen?"

Mellie swallowed, feeling tears pricking at the back on her eyes. Years ago, when her own family had shunned her after the broken betrothal, Elizabeth had saved her by giving her a place to live and a purpose.

Mellie would sacrifice anything—her future, her happiness—for the Queen.

"I would," she answered hoarsely. "Besides—"

Her breath caught on an unexpected sob, and she shook her head, trying in vain to keep two fat tears from sliding from the corners of each eye.

"Besides," she managed to continue, "once he finds out who I am, he'll ken I betrayed him."

She would just be one more woman who chose another over him.

Brigit was silent for a long while, then took a deep breath. "Do ye love him?"

"I do."

The words were out of Mellie's lips before she even thought about it, but she knew it was true. The shock of that truth left her gasping, and her tears halting, as her eyes widened.

"I do love him," she whispered again in astonishment. "*Mon Dieu*, I love him!"

Her maid hummed thoughtfully, then shrugged.

"Well," she said with a sigh, "that makes things more difficult, does it no'?"

Mellie just shook her head, too astonished to reply.

Somewhere over the last fortnight, in between seeing Lachlan lead his clan, love his daughter, and treat her with respect, Mellie had fallen in love with him.

Dieu l'aide, but she loved Lachlan.

What she was about to do might hurt him, might betray him, but she'd willingly give up a chance at future happiness if it saved his life.

The Crown *had* to know he was innocent, and she'd sacrifice her chance at love for that.

But she wouldn't leave without showing him how much he'd come to mean to her.

She lifted her chin once more, straightening her shoulders and meeting Brigit's gaze. "Ready a bath for me. Have supper sent up here for both of us. We're going to pack, as I will be leaving before dawn."

Brigit curtsied and grinned. "And the bath, milady?"

Mellie took a deep breath and stood. "Tonight, I'm going to him."

CHAPTER 10

The moon was rising over the mountains.

Lachlan lay in bed, his hands stacked behind his head, and gazed through the closer of the two sets of windows in the laird's chambers. He'd never cared for this room when it had belonged to his parents, then his brother… but he had to admit the view was stunning.

When he'd become laird, he'd been nigh overwhelmed with his new responsibilities, which was one of the reasons he'd requested his friend and kinsman, Ross, to return from Scone to aid him. Between Ross and Owen's support—as well as the trick of listening to Gillepatric and doing the exact opposite of whatever the man recommended—Lachlan had not only preserved his clan's future, but had gained their respect and love.

He told himself that was enough.

But more and more lately, visions of blue eyes teased him, promising him *more*.

He was betrothed to the woman, but he doubted he really *knew* her yet.

The soft knock at his door startled him, but wasn't altogether unexpected. He glanced down at himself to make sure he was completely covered, knowing sometimes if Simone couldn't sleep, she'd sneak out of the nursery and seek him out. He'd be damned if he was going to start wearing braies to sleep, so he always made sure his manly bits were tucked in.

"Come in, sweetheart," he called, wondering if she'd had a bad dream.

But when the door opened, it wasn't his daughter who stepped inside.

Slowly, Lachlan sat up, the coverlet falling away from his chest.

"*Mellie?*" he choked out in surprise.

In the light from the candle she held, he could see her wide lips lift in a teasing grin. "Ye mean, ye didnae expect me? Ye were hoping for *another* 'sweetheart' then?"

As she lifted the hem of her robe and kicked the door shut behind her, Lachlan shook his head. "I— I thought ye were Simone. What are ye doing here?"

In response, she lifted the candle away from her body, allowing him to see more of her. Her golden hair had recently been washed and fell in curls around her shoulders. Her skin seemed to gleam, and her curves were…

Well, her curves were barely contained in a silk robe, which looked as if it had been spun from moonbeams. It shimmered silver in the light coming through the window, and made the rest of her look as if she were some kind of fairy princess.

"*God's Blood,*" he whispered, but didn't realize he had, until her smile grew.

"Aye, Lachlan," she all but purred, as she started across the room to the large bed. "We are betrothed, are we no'? And ye cannae deny ye're no' against a betrothed couple sharing a bed."

Nay, he couldn't. His daughter was proof of that, wasn't she?

But he'd vowed not to allow another woman to hurt him the way Alice had. She'd left him.

Would Mellie one day do the same?

Unable to drag his eyes away from the way the silk molded to her, as she bent to place the candle on the table beside the bed, Lachlan shook his head. "I've been aching for ye, lass," he finally confessed, deciding truth would serve them best. "But I didnae want ye to be obligated to me."

She straightened and raised a brow. "Really? Because as I see it, I owe *ye* a release. *Le petit mort.*"

Before he could do more than open his mouth, she reached for the tie at her waist, and then the moonlit silk was trailing off her shoulders to pool at her feet.

And Lachlan sat there, gaping like a fish, as he drank in the sight of his betrothed's gorgeous, *nude* body.

"*Jesu Christo,* lass," he finally managed, shifting, as his cock tried to jump to readiness beneath the heavy coverlets. "Ye cannae mean—"

"Oh, I do." Bending, she crawled onto the bed, then shifted, so her weight rested on one knee. "I verra much want—"

"Stop." Shaking his head, Lachlan's eyes lit on the little pucker of the arrow wound on her shoulder, and that—more than anything else—helped get his desire under control. He knew so little about her. "*Stop,*" he growled again, not allowing himself to look at her, to reach for her. "I told ye, I don' want ye to *offer* yerself, to be obligated. I'll no' deny yer questions or favors, Mellie. Just donae make this feel *cheap.*"

Cheap.

The word hung between them for a long, silent moment, and Lachlan resisted the urge to close his eyes.

Finally, he felt the mattress move as she shifted, pulling

her knees up in front of her and wrapping her arms around them.

"I donae ken how to make it feel any other way," she whispered.

And his heart damn near broke.

"Lachlan, what ye did for me…"

When she trailed off, he finally gave up the fight, gave up his good intentions, and glanced at her. What he saw nearly did him in.

She looked…*lost*. Alone, definitely.

His palms itched to reach for her, to gather her in his arms, to *love her*.

"Ye don' have to say it, Mellie," he offered in a gentle voice, shifting his own weight under the wool coverlet.

Funny. They were both on his bed, nude as the day they were born, but Lachlan's attention wasn't on making love to her.

It was on the way her smile seemed sad when she finally met his eyes. The way she hunched her shoulders, as if she could protect herself, even though *she* was the one to bare her body to his gaze.

"What ye did for me, Lachlan, nae man has ever done. Nae man has ever cared about my pleasure. I…" She trailed off, shook her head, then focused her attention on the blue wool coverlet between them. She took a deep breath. "I want ye. I want to please ye. *I* want that."

Dark eyes met his, and he saw the truth in them.

"I *want* to please ye, Lachlan, nae because I think it's what ye expect, but because it's what would please *me*."

Dear God in Heaven.

With a groan, Lachlan dropped back against the pillows, throwing one arm across his eyes. "Ye're killing me, lass," he ground out through his clenched jaw. "I had the best of intentions, and then ye go and say something like *that*."

She snorted softly. "Ye ken ye're the only man who's withstood my attempts at seduction?"

For a moment, Lachlan wondered just how many men there'd been before him. But he dismissed the thought, because her past didn't matter to him.

Only her future.

If they married, all that mattered would be the knowledge *he'd* be the only man in her bed. Forever.

"When I was seventeen, my father betrothed me to a powerful laird in the Western Isles."

She began her story in a low voice, and Lachlan peeked out from under his forearm. She was still sitting with her arms wrapped around her knees, her ankles crossed, but she was staring out the window at the moon.

He didn't interrupt.

"My father and the laird—I'll no' say his name, so donae ask—agreed on a date the following year. He took me to his keep so I could get used to the way his clan did things, he said." She shrugged. "It was no' so different from my life at home, and I was excited about being a grand lady of a powerful clan."

She lapsed into silence, obviously lost in her memories. Lachlan moved his arm away from his eyes and laced his fingers behind his head once more. He didn't want to sit up again—didn't want to do anything to interrupt her.

For the first time since the Queen had betrothed them, he thought mayhap he was seeing the true Melisandre Lamond.

Finally, she took a deep breath and continued, "Aye, I would've been content with my life there, for I enjoyed the benefits. My betrothed took me to bed, claiming 'twas his right to try me out. I didnae even mind that; sometimes I'd even find pleasure in his arms, which was nice enough." She paused, then glanced his way. "Then I fell pregnant."

The parallels between her history and his own caused

Lachlan to catch his breath. He remembered his reaction when Alice had told him she was pregnant, and wondered if Mellie's betrothed had done the same.

"What did he say?" he whispered, needing to know.

One side of her lips tugged upward, and the shoulder on that side lifted in a half-shrug. "He was pleased, since it proved I would make a fine wife." Then her expression sobered, her eyes staring *through* Lachlan. "Until I lost the bairn. I was more than halfway through the pregnancy at that point—a bitter winter—and there was so much pain. And blood." Her voice fell to a whisper. "So much pain."

Lachlan closed his eyes on his own pain, his heart breaking for her, even as his palms itched to reach for her.

"I'm sorry, lass," he whispered.

She hadn't seemed to hear him.

"What was worse, was after. My betrothed told me, since I couldnae carry a bairn to term, I was of nae use to him. He broke the contract and sent me home."

His eyes bulging wide, Lachlan clenched his jaw to keep from growling in anger.

She seemed to sense his outrage, and nodded as she exhaled and met his gaze sadly. "My parents blamed me for the loss of a powerful alliance, and there was talk of sending me to a nunnery. But then the missive came from Scone, the Queen inviting me to court to become one of her ladies. My father told me I was to keep my mouth shut about my shame, that if the Queen didnae ken yet, mayhap there was still hope for me."

Behind his head, Lachlan's hands closed into fists around his hair, tugging to give himself something else to focus on besides her pain.

"Ye see why I am loyal to Queen Elizabeth?"

"Aye lass," he croaked out.

She held his gaze. "I want ye to remember that, Lachlan."

He didn't understand what she was saying, but this was the most serious he'd ever seen her. "Have ye seen yer family since ye went to Scone?"

She shook her head. "They're dead to me. And as for my ex-betrothed...?" Her shrug was one-sided again. "I've heard he's finally married." One side of her lips lifted again wryly. "When ye told me of yer Alice, I wondered if mayhap they'd found one another."

Well *that* suggestion startled a bark of laughter out of him. " 'Twould be fitting!"

Her smile faded.

"Ye ken what I wish, Lachlan?" she whispered. He shook his head, mesmerized by her blue gaze.

"I wish... I wish..." She shook her head, and glanced away, focusing on the coverlet between them, then took a deep breath. "I wish we were already married, so when I rip everything open and show ye my real self, ye might—"

Dark eyes flashed his way, then away again.

To hell with his intentions! He hated this uncertainty in her voice.

Lachlan slowly pushed himself upright. "I might what, lass?"

"Ye might hold me," she whispered.

There was no way he could deny her that. Not now.

With a sigh, he spread his hands, palms out, inviting her in.

With a sound suspiciously like a sob, she threw herself against his chest, in a flash of skin and breasts and more skin. Lachlan felt like an arse for noticing, when she was so obviously hurting, but he was still a man.

A very stiff man.

And within moments, she was snuggled up against him under the coverlet, his arm around her, and her cheek pillowed against his chest. He lay flat on his back and stared up at the bed hangings, trying in vain to convince his cock that the tits and hips and *curves* pressed against his side meant naught.

It didn't work.

"Lachlan?" she whispered against his skin. "I lied."

Frowning, he dragged his gaze sideways, finding hers in the candlelight. Under one of her hands, his heartbeat sped up.

Lied?

Was she finally going to confess why she was here?

But her expression melted into a sad smile again, and he knew she was speaking of something more recent. "While I appreciate the hug, and have been hoping for it for days, 'tisnae what I meant to say."

"About wishes?"

She dropped her chin, in what might've been a nod, had she not been pressed against him, and focused her gaze on her finger, which was making slow, maddening circles over his chest.

"Now that I'm here with ye, I wish I was a better woman. I wish I didnae ken *how* to seduce a man, so I wouldnae ken the shame of failing with ye. I wish I had been able to come to ye, as a woman might who was falling in love with a man, and have him believe her."

Lachlan stiffened, trying to make sense of that convoluted sentence.

Was she saying…she was falling in love with him?

He turned his attention back to the bed hangings, wondering if that's what he hoped for, or feared.

"Ye ken what I wish, Mellie?" He scrubbed his hand across his face, but didn't wait for her to respond. "I wish that complete bastard had never taught ye that lesson."

When she lifted her head from his shoulder, he glanced at her and saw she didn't understand.

"I wish he'd never taught ye—never let ye think—that yer only worth came from yer body. Yer ability to please him—or any man! Yer ability to bear a child."

He rolled to face her, shifting his hold on her so she fit against him more snugly. They were now lying nose to nose, her blue eyes close to his. When he inhaled, he breathed in *Mellie*.

" 'Tis what ye thought happened with Alice, is it no'?" he whispered gruffly. "Ye were surprised when I told ye the truth; that it was her choice to leave. Ye thought I'd sent her away?"

She held his gaze. "Aye. I did."

"Ye had reason to think that, because of what that bastard did to ye."

"There's a woman at court, Isabel de Strathbogie. She was supposed to marry the king's brother."

He dropped his chin slightly. "I remember. She has a son."

"Aye, Alex. Elizabeth dotes on him, and the lad will never want for aught, despite the way his father neglected his mother."

Lachlan exhaled. "Ye're trying to point out that what happened to ye is common? For a man to put aside a betrothal and ruin a woman's life?"

She didn't reply. She didn't have to.

He tried a different line of reasoning. "When yer betrothed broke the contract, he was saying ye had no value. Ye believed him, did ye no'?"

Again, she didn't reply, but he saw her wince.

"Ye came to believe yer worth was only in yer body. In how well ye could please a man." His voice turned hoarse. "Ye forgot about yer quick wit and sharp intelligence. And yer protective nature. And yer ability with a set of oars and a dagger. Ye forgot about yer *caring*."

He pulled her closer, until his forehead was pressed

against hers. Until *he* was pressed against her, with her hands trapped against his chest and his stiff cock pushing against her soft thigh.

"Ye are the most caring person I ken, Mellie," he whispered gruffly. "Ye care enough to get to ken people here at An Torr. Ye care about Simone. Ye—" He closed his eyes. "Ye care about me. But no' as much as I care about ye."

She jerked away from him, pulling herself up on one elbow. "What?"

He took a deep breath and met her eyes, hating this feeling of uncertainty. He hated feeling vulnerable, hated knowing this might all come to naught.

But he also knew, no matter how much this hurt *him*, to bare his soul, she needed to hear it.

"I love ye, Melisandre. Ye're an amazing woman. How could I *no'* love ye?"

Something shifted in her eyes then, incredulity turned to sorrow. Her lips pulled up on one side.

"For all the right reasons?"

Despite his cock pressed between them, he nodded. "The *only* reasons."

Her smile slowly grew. And although her joy didn't *quite* reach her eyes, she looked happier than she'd been since they'd begun the conversation.

Sinking back against him, she reached one arm around him, caressing the sensitive skin down his flank. "Then I guess we're back where we started."

Distracted by her touch, Lachlan could do little more than grunt inquisitively.

"Ye're a rare and wonderful man, Lachlan Fraser. Ye make me feel *good*, and I want to share all that I am with ye."

It was her words, more than the way her hand slid around to cup his backside, which had him grinning. "*All* of ye, lass?"

Her grin turned lewd as she rocked her pelvis forward,

catching his cock between her thighs. "All the best parts at least."

God's Blood, but it was getting hard to think with her all... all...*all* in his arms.

"As nice as this is, 'tisnae the best parts—" he began gruffly, but she interrupted him when she began to chuckle.

"How could I no' love ye, Lachlan? Ye force me to be a better woman."

"Ye're the best I ken, Mellie."

"Aye." She pushed herself up, bracing herself over him, as her hair fell in a curtain around them. "The *verra* best."

And then she rolled atop him, his hands came up to grasp her hips, and he gave up battling the inevitable.

This kiss was...

Well, it was likely *the verra best*, as she'd said, but Lachlan couldn't seem to focus on her lips, even when her tongue rasped against his and sent a bolt of pure desire to his aching bollocks.

Nay, the reason he couldn't concentrate on the kiss, was because of everything else he was trying to concentrate on at the same time.

Her breasts pressed against his chest, and his hands instinctively slid up her side to cup them. Without breaking their kiss, he slid his hands under them, his thumbs finding her nipples.

Despite her claims the last time he'd touched her thusly—when she'd told him not to touch her tits—she moaned deep in her throat and wriggled enticingly against him.

His cock was pressed between them, until the moment she pulled her lips away from his and slid her thighs off either side of his own. *Now* his stiff member was pressed against the curls at the juncture of her legs, straining upward, as if it knew where it wanted to be.

And Mellie rocked backward, her hands leaving his

shoulders to skim down his stomach, as she stared at his cock.

"*Sainte Vierge*, Lachlan!"

He chuckled, his palms caressing the parts of her he could reach. "I doubt the Virgin mother would appreciate the comparison."

She didn't acknowledge his joke, her gaze still on his stiff member. "I've never…" When she rocked forward, then back, Lachlan let his head fall back with a groan of pleasure. "I've never seen one so large."

And *then* her hands closed around it, her fingers not able to circle the blasted thing, and Lachlan *knew* he'd died and gone to Heaven. She began to stroke, even as she rocked, and he focused his gaze on the bed hangings and tried to keep from spilling all over her hands.

God alone—or possibly the Sainted Virgin, as Mellie was fond of evoking—knew how long she stroked him. Lachlan's grip on her thighs had turned hard, and his breathing harsh, as he tried to control himself.

Was this repayment for the pleasure he'd shown her?

Did she *want* him to spill?

And then she shifted, leaning forward and lifting herself, before positioning his cock under her opening.

When she sank down atop his swollen member, they both groaned in satisfaction.

"So big, Lachlan," she gasped, her back arching. "*Bon Dieu*, so big!"

Unable to resist the temptation, he flexed his hips, thrusting himself even deeper in her tightness. He knew he was a large man—all over—but there was something so erotic about her praise.

"Lass," he all but growled, "ye feel so blasted good."

Her wetness, her perfection, encompassed him. He

wanted to flip her over, to sink into her again and again…but he wouldn't.

"Find yer pleasure, lass," he gasped. "Set the pace."

The grin she gave him, the look of wonder in her eyes, told him he'd made the right offer, despite the brittle control it had taken. But then she dropped her hands to his thighs, rocking forward and back the same as before, only this time, *on his cock*, and he decided letting her lead had its advantages.

She rode him.

She rode him gently at first, then hard. When she shifted forward—her eyes glazed and her breaths coming in pants—and braced her hands against his chest, he grabbed her hips and began to help in her efforts. She rose off his cock, then a heartbeat later, slammed back down, until they were both grunting with pleasure.

The familiar pressure was building behind his bollocks, and he knew he wasn't going to last much longer. Thinking he needed her to find her release soon, he thought to reach for her pearl to help her along, when she suddenly leaned forward.

With her hands braced on the mattress on either side of him, she took her weight off his pelvis, allowing *him* to do the thrusting. They were both sweating in the most wonderful way, and he didn't think he'd ever seen anything so erotic as her curls cascading down around them, as her tits bounced so near his mouth.

His grip on her hips tightened, and despite his intention to make sure she found her fulfillment ahead of him, his intention to let her set the pace, he couldn't seem to make himself stop thrusting into her tight wetness.

And the fact she was moaning his name didn't help.

He knew he was close.

"Mellie?" he gasped, forcing himself to freeze, to meet her eyes.

She was the one to finish the move, to sink down on him. She lowered herself until her chest was plastered against his, even as her hips made small movements over him.

Was she even aware of what she was doing?

"Please, Lachlan," she whispered.

And when he met her eyes, he saw something there.

Desperation?

God's Blood, he needed her to find release, and soon, because he was sorely lacking in control when it came to her!

Suddenly, he remembered what had triggered her release last time.

With her plastered against him this way, his cock buried deep inside her, he reached both hands up and around, resting on her arse cheeks.

Moaning, she closed her eyes, tilting her hips back so she glided along his cock, even as she thrust her bottom into his hands.

And when his fingers brushed against the puckered, sensitive entrance, she went frantic.

With a wild cry, she burst into motion, sliding back and forth on his cock. Trying to control his own breathing, and knowing he was failing, Lachlan used one finger to caress the puckered circle, then press ever so gently, ever so slightly, inside.

Her release exploded around his cock, as she stiffened and thrust her head back. With closed eyes, she screamed his name, as her wet, tight muscles spasmed around him.

And Lachlan gave up the fight.

With a roar to match her own, he spilled his seed against her womb, the sudden warmth making him feel both shame and a fierce sort of pride.

After, she collapsed in his arms, and he gently disentangled them. They didn't speak, but she stretched out beside him and rested her head on his chest.

Her lips brushed against his skin as their breathing slowed, and he captured her hand in his.

God's Wounds, but that was the most wonderful thing he'd ever done.

A better experience than he'd ever had with any other woman.

The verra best, she'd said.

As his eyes closed, Lachlan was smiling.

She was right.

∽

Mellie's hands shook as she placed the note on the table beside the candle which had long ago burnt out.

It'd been hours since she'd fallen asleep in Lachlan's arms, but her rest had been brief. She'd gathered up the expensive robe, then had snuck from the room, as Lachlan continued to slumber.

Brigit had been waiting for her, and Mellie had quickly changed into her riding clothes. Court had been the one to teach her about the benefits of trewes, even under a gown, and Mellie had every intention of riding hard and fast.

The way she'd ridden Lachlan, only hours ago.

She flushed, her pulse quickening at the reminder of the incredible orgasm she'd experienced. The incredible pleasure *he'd* given her.

Given her.

No man had ever *given her* pleasure. No man had ever cared enough to learn what gave her pleasure, and then done it, no matter how unusual.

I love ye, Melisandre. How could I no'?

His words had echoed in her mind and her heart all

evening. He loved her, as she loved him, and now she had to betray him.

Nay. Ye do this to protect *him. He might never understand it as such, no' after what Alice did to him, but ye* will *keep him safe.*

Her letter said none of this.

My love,
You have given me more than I ever expected to find. When you spoke of my best parts, I know what you meant, and my heart will never be the same.

You hold it, Lachlan. No matter what happens, remember that. Tell Simone I will always love her.

I am sorry.
M.

In the moonlight, he looked near angelic, his light brown hair glowing almost silver. Her palms itched to brush it out of his eyes, but she held back, not knowing how deep a sleeper he was.

She couldn't afford to be stopped now.

Not when she was so close to forsaking her vows to the Queen—to her fellow angels—and staying here at An Torr with this man forever.

With a muffled sob, she whirled for the door.

If she didn't leave now, she might never leave; might never be *able* to leave.

And Lachlan—and the Frasers of Lovat—depended on her to convince the Crown he was innocent of treason.

Although he'd never know her real reason for being

assigned his betrothal, for coming to An Torr, for trying to seduce him, Mellie knew she was doing the right thing.

Even if she'd lost her heart along the way.

She closed the door to the laird's chambers softly behind her, allowing her forehead to fall against the wood.

Sainte Vierge, pray for me!

Her heart was breaking, but she couldn't allow her tears to fall. She had to slip into the nursery, to kiss Simone goodbye. Even if the lassie didn't know, Mellie had to see her, touch her, one last time.

And then she had to ride for Scone.

She had to forsake her future with Lachlan.

She had to betray her heart.

CHAPTER 11

*L*ife at An Torr became hell, and it was all thanks to its laird.

When Lachlan awoke the morning after the best sex of his life, he was disappointed to realize a naked Mellie was no longer curled up beside him. He didn't think anyone —servants or nay—would begrudge the two of them what they'd done last night, since they were betrothed.

But apparently, Mellie hadn't wanted to be found in his bed, and had snuck back to her own chambers without him realizing.

Still, he didn't bother hiding his cheer that morning, to the point where Owen rolled his eyes, and said, "I retract my previous accusations. 'Tis clear ye've only just now bedded the lass."

Lachlan merely laughed.

He wanted to see her that morning—to hold her, to taste her again—but she hadn't yet emerged from her room, and he didn't want to wake her. There'd be plenty of future mornings where he could watch her sleep and kiss her awake.

The thought of mornings, days, *years* with Mellie had him grinning all morning.

It wasn't until noon he realized something was wrong.

He was training with the men in the fields, and when he was through, found a worried-looking Simone waiting for him. Usually his daughter lacked the patience to stand around for so long, so he knew something was amiss.

Squatting before her, he offered a smile. "What is it, sweetheart?"

"I cannae find Mellie," Simone said bluntly. "I wanted to go fishing again—just from the shore this time—and went to see if she'd come with me. But she's no' in her room."

Lachlan shrugged, as he stood once more and offered her his hand. "Mayhap she's finally breaking her fast? She must've slept a long time."

He managed to keep the pride from his tone, though just barely.

They were walking back to the keep, and he saw Simone shake her head, the frown still on her little lips. "Her maid isnae in her chambers either, but all of her trunks are packed."

Lachlan's grin faded. "Really?"

When his daughter glanced up at him, he saw how serious her gray eyes were. "Aye."

They both hurried their steps.

When Lachlan reached Mellie's chamber, he pushed the door open without knocking. The maid wasn't there, as Simone had said, and Mellie's baggage was all carefully stacked along one wall.

As if she were readying to leave on a journey.

Readying to leave *him*.

"Go find Ella," he commanded in a hoarse voice.

"But, Da—"

"Donae argue!" He realized he was taking out his worry

on his daughter, and dragged his gaze away from the empty room and what he was afraid it represented. "I love ye, Simone, but I need ye in the nursery for a bit. Go, please."

Her gray eyes were wide with her own worry, but she nodded solemnly and dropped his hand. She turned to walk away, but changed her mind and threw her arms around his middle, just briefly.

"I love ye too, Da," she whispered, looking up at him. "And I love Mellie. Promise ye'll find her?"

It should be a simple thing to swear, to find Mellie. But something about this room, something about the sinking feeling in his stomach, told Lachlan it wouldn't be that easy.

Still, he cleared his throat as he patted his daughter's shoulder.

"I promise," he managed to say.

And he knew, in that moment, he *would*.

He'd waited his entire life for her, and no matter what it took, he'd find her.

And if she didn't want a future with him—if everything they'd shared had been a complete lie, part of that first seduction, well then…

Lachlan slowly inhaled.

Well, he needed to know that too.

"Martin!" he bellowed, as he whirled away from the open door and stalked in the opposite direction. "Martin! Find Brigit! I would speak to her about her mistress!"

When the seneschal called out his acknowledgment, Lachlan headed for his chamber. 'Twas the last place he'd seen her, and mayhap there was something there.

There was.

The letter was a small piece of parchment, folded in half and tucked under a cup, on his bedside table. Lachlan realized he was staring down at it, his hands curled into fists at his sides, a sense of dread slithering in his gut.

'Tisnae an adder!

Then why was he afraid?

With a muttered curse, he reached for the letter and opened it.

It began with *My love*, and told him everything he'd been hoping *and* dreading.

Mellie loved him. That much was clear from her words; she hadn't lied.

But she was gone, and didn't say where she was going. Not only that, it sounded as if she expected it to be a permanent absence.

He was proud of how steady his hands were, as he folded the parchment once more and tucked it into the pouch at his belt.

He loved her.

He loved Mellie, and she claimed to still love him, which meant, whatever had taken her away from An Torr, was serious.

Taking a deep breath, Lachlan lifted his gaze out the window.

How long ago had she left?

It mattered not. He *would* find her.

"Martin!" he bellowed again, as he whirled away from the view.

They discovered Brigit hiding in the kitchens. She sat on the cook's bed, in the little alcove behind the hearth, her knees drawn up to her chest. When she saw she'd been discovered—and looked into the face of Lachlan's anger—she untangled herself and stood with a sigh.

The cheeky little maid placed one hand on her hip and cocked her head at him. "She went to Scone, to the Queen, milord."

"How long?" he snapped, not entirely surprised.

"Before dawn. 'Twas a full moon."

Aye, he remembered.

"Did this have to do with the letter from her friend she received yesterday?"

Brigit shrugged. " 'Tis likely."

Which meant Mellie had already known she would be leaving when she'd come to Lachlan's room last night.

He frowned, irritated at himself.

Of course she knew she'd be leaving. 'Twas why she came!

She'd known she'd be leaving him, leaving An Torr, and she'd come to his room one last time, not to seduce him, but to make him understand her feelings. She'd told him of her past, had *ripped herself open*—as she'd described it—and bared her soul to him.

And in return, he'd loved her.

Unconsciously, his hand hovered over the pouch where he'd placed her letter.

You hold my heart.

By God's Wounds, she held *his* heart, and he wasn't going to let her escape with it.

His attention focused once more on Brigit, who still stood in front of him expectantly.

"What else?" he growled.

The little maid clucked her tongue. "She told me to prepare her luggage, but didnae forbid me to tell ye where she's going." The lass grinned. "Ye could still catch her."

"Aye," he agreed, as he whirled away from her. "Unpack yer mistress's things. I'll be bringing her back."

It was his promise to himself, no matter what awaited him in Scone.

Easier said than done.

A fast horse would get him to Scone in three days. He wasn't sure how hard Mellie was pushing *her* mount, but even if she were running from him, it wouldn't be too hard to catch her. He rode into the night, only stopping when it became too dark to see, but was back up before dawn to continue on.

He might've caught her by Dunkeld, had his horse not gone lame.

Cursing himself for a fool, and a blasted idiot for pushing his mount so hard, Lachlan walked beside the limping animal to the nearest town...which took hours.

And the whole time, he pictured Mellie riding farther and farther away from him.

Of course, he had to admit it was possible she wasn't running *from* him at all.

Brigit had said she was going to Scone Palace, to see the Queen. Not for the first time, on that lonely road, with the sun beating down, Lachlan wondered who she actually was.

Not in her heart, because he thought he knew *that*.

But what her role at court really was.

She clearly was a confidante to the Queen; not just as a lady-in-waiting, but also as a friend.

The Queen had specifically chosen Mellie to travel to An Torr as his betrothed.

Mellie purposefully pretended to be someone she wasn't —cold and haughty—in order to color his opinion of her. And she not only tried to seduce him, but even hinted later it was something she was used to doing.

Had the Queen sent her to seduce *him*?

For what purpose?

And how was all this tied to the confrontation in the

alleyway so many weeks ago, or to the turmoil at court, just before he'd left to return home?

Lachlan had to eventually admit he wouldn't be able to answer these questions, at least not until he got to Scone or caught up with her along the way. And at the rate he was currently traveling, it would take much longer than he'd hoped.

Eventually, he reached a town where he could trade horses, and by pushing both himself and the new animal, then buying another one, he made good time. The lost hours —both on the morning before knowing she'd left, and the time he'd spent walking—might hurt him, but if she hadn't been riding too hard, he might still have a chance.

Oh, he'd asked at each town and inn he'd stopped at, and some *did* remember seeing a beautiful golden-haired woman who rode like the very Devil was on her tail. Lachlan could imagine she'd be memorable, and the sightings indicated he was getting closer.

By the time he reached the outskirts of Scone, he calculated he was less than an hour behind her, and if she had slowed once she entered the city—which he did not—he might even catch her before she reached the Palace.

Of course, he knew where she was going, and knew who she'd see once she arrived. If he had to, he'd camp outside the Queen's throne room, until the woman allowed him access to his betrothed, however long that would take.

The betrothed, who may or may not *actually* be his betrothed, depending on why the Queen sent her to An Torr in the first place.

Nay, I signed that contract, as did Her Majesty.

No matter the reason Mellie had been at An Torr, their betrothal was valid.

And he loved the woman, by God's Wounds!

Which was why, mayhap, he could feel her ahead of him.

As he impatiently nudged his way through the over-crowded streets, cursing and calling out to get people and carts to make way and let him through, he could swear she was just ahead of him, waiting.

They were connected somehow.

He knew it.

And it was that intuition, that *connection*, which grabbed him by the heart and *shook him* when he heard the shouts from up ahead, and realized the tide of people had turned and were heading *away* from the large square in front of him.

Somehow, he *knew* she was the cause. She was in the center of that panic, and that meant she was in trouble.

Knowing the mass of people blocking his path would make maneuvering more difficult, Lachlan prayed his horse didn't knock down any innocent bystanders as he battled his way toward the source of the screams. Miraculously, a path opened ahead of him, and he reached for his sword.

The square loomed ahead, with the Palace looming even further in the distance, and he could see a tight knot of people struggling on the opposite side. And in the midst of it all, was a head of thick golden curls and a swirling skirt.

He kicked his horse into a gallop and drew his blade, bellowing her name.

CHAPTER 12

Mayhap she got complacent.

Mayhap she was simply so deeply distracted, her mind and heart miles away, back in An Torr.

All the saints in Heaven likely knew how little she'd wanted to leave An Torr; how little she'd wanted to leave Lachlan and Simone.

If Lachlan came after her—and she both feared and hoped for that, in equal parts—she doubted her ability to follow through with her mission.

All he'd have to do is take her in his arms, stare down at her with those too-understanding gray eyes, and say something kind and wonderful and loving.

And she'd be doomed. She'd completely forsake her fellow Angels, her friends at court, and the very mission her Queen had given her, if it meant making Lachlan happy.

Which is why she'd ridden so hard and so fast, ensuring she put enough distance between them.

But by the time she reached Scone, there'd been no sign of him. So aye, mayhap she'd grown complacent.

When she'd at last reached Scone, the crush of people—at once so familiar, and so foreign, after all the weeks at An Torr—had forced her off her horse. So instead of rushing through the city, she was carefully leading the large animal through the main streets and smaller squares, until she could see the Palace's crenellations.

And she hadn't been paying as close attention as she should've been, because Lachlan catching up to her wasn't the *only* danger.

It was the point of a dagger in her back which had her freezing, wondering which of the crowd around her intended to rob her, even as she cursed her inattentiveness.

"No' a sound, lass," growled a man's voice in her ear, the scent of onions washing over her with the words. "Drop the reins to that fine animal."

The horse?

That's all they wanted?

Well, she could afford to lose her mount this close to the Palace, if it kept her moving closer to her destination.

She dropped the reins.

But instead of withdrawing, the man behind her shoved the dagger in even further, until the tip of the blade cut through her traveling kirtle and pricked against the skin beneath, causing her to suck in a sharp breath.

"Don' make a sound," the voice growled again, as the man nudged her forward. "Come with us."

Us?

Mellie's mind churned frantically as she stumbled, wishing she had some hint of Rosa's intellect or Court's battle ability. "Us" meant there was more than one, and wanting her to go with them meant they had other plans, rather than a mere robbery.

"Ye can have the horse," she hissed, knowing the longer

they stood in the square, while the crowds flowed around them, the more chance there was of someone growing suspicious.

A heavy hand came down on her shoulder, simultaneously steering her toward the shadows between two buildings, and pulling her back against his blade.

"Aye," Onion-Breath said, "an' I told ye no' to speak. We're getting a nice purse for killing ye and making it look like a cutpurse attack, but there's nae reason we can' enjoy ye a bit first."

The last was said with a leer, as the man pushed her on. Mellie wasn't as scared by the threat as she suspected he'd intended she be. She was an *Angel*, and that meant she'd gotten into—and out of, thank God—worse situations.

It was the casual reference to someone *paying* these men —how many were there?—to kill her, which had given her pause.

"Someone wants me dead?" she asked in a low voice, hoping to keep the man talking, even as she pretended to stumble.

The man simply yanked her upright, the blade nicking her flesh again, as he huffed impatiently.

"Shut yer mouth! At least until we're ready to use it," he added, with a crude chuckle.

And that's when Mellie knew her time was up. They were almost to the edge of the square, where there were fewer people. The shadows of an alleyway loomed ahead, and she knew she had to act. Out here, she had the advantage of the crowd, and the odds in her favor someone may step in to help, but in there…?

Years ago, Court had taught them about fighting in close quarters. She'd also instructed Mellie and Rosa 'twas usually better to scream and make noise and attract attention, even under threat of harm, than to allow a man to drag her away. If the man stabbed her before he ran from her rescuers, well then…at least she had a better chance of getting help right away, and a better chance of survival.

Court's trainings flashed through Mellie's brain in just the short time it took for her to draw a deep breath. Before Onion-Breath knew what she was about, she threw herself forward, wrenching out of his grasp, and began to scream for all she was worth.

Some of it was wordless, but she made sure there were also enough words of "Help! Help!" to draw attention.

As she hit the ground, rolled, and came up in a crouch, the man cursed. She'd gotten out of his hold without further harm, and now she had to get, and stay, away from him.

Scrambling upright, she lunged forward, but felt a hand close around her wrist and yank her sideways.

Merde!

She'd forgotten he had accomplices!

And rather than coming to her rescue, her screams seemed to have induced some sort of human stampede. All around her, people fled from the square, even as Mellie struggled to get away from her captor.

The man yanked hard, and she stumbled against a foul-smelling, dirty body. Pretending to slump in defeat, Mellie used those precious few seconds to fumble for her boot and the needle-blade dagger she kept hidden there.

Sainte Vierge! Keep me safe!

Thanks be to Mother Mary, her blade easily pulled free of her boot, and she slashed upward. The dagger was made for stabbing, but her awkward swipe seemed effective enough, as the man cursed and released her, dropping her to her hands and knees once more.

Mellie scrambled forward, but someone grabbed her

ankle before she could get very far. She kicked backward without looking and heard a man grunt in pain.

All around her, people were yelling, and feet and wagons went thundering by as they moved away from the fight. Mellie did her best to reach the safety of the crowd, but it seemed to thin, even as she stumbled to her feet, praying for help.

Suddenly, a roar filled the air, startling them all.

Mellie wasn't the only one to turn to the far side of the square, but she was likely the only one who ran *toward* the gorgeous man in Fraser plaid, sitting atop a massive horse.

Lachlan!

She couldn't breathe, her lungs having become frozen from the terror of knowing she had been—still might?—be killed. But even the lack of air wouldn't keep her from rushing toward the man she loved, especially when he was shouting her name.

Still astride his horse, Lachlan brandished his sword, and bellowed, "*Mellie!*"

And in that moment, Mellie knew she had never heard anything sweeter.

He reached her at the same time someone else grabbed her arm from behind. Ignoring the enemy for a heartbeat, she watched as Lachlan threw himself from his horse, his blade already swinging, before she decided to turn back to the man holding her in an attempt to break free.

But she never got the chance to move.

Lachlan pulled her out of the other man's grip and up against himself, tucking her face against his shoulder with his free hand, as he slashed behind her with his sword, and the pressure on her arm went slack.

Mellie took a moment to inhale deeply of his scent—how had she ever thought she could leave him?—before the screaming penetrated her mind, and she peeked back.

The man who had grabbed her—the same man who'd had the dagger, which had dug into her back, though now was lying useless on the ground—was now clutching at the end his shoulder, where his arm had been only moments before.

"Are ye hurt?" Lachlan asked in a growl , as he pushed her behind him, keeping his attention on the other bandits, who had fanned out before his blade.

Mellie had time to whisper, "Nay, thank the Virgin and ye," before she settled her back against his and faced the men who had circled behind them.

She held her dagger at the ready, the way Court had taught her all those years before, but inside she was shaking.

Now it wasn't just her own safety she was worried about, but Lachlan's as well.

∼

By all the saints in Heaven, Lachlan didn't think he'd *ever* forget the terror of seeing her running, *reaching* for him, only to be yanked back. He'd gone a bit mad then, but the threat was far from over.

Now she stood at his back, while the bandits circled them, and everyone else fled. There were six of the enemy left, and each eyed him, sizing up the threat he presented.

A threat?

Nay, he vowed.

He would be *their end*.

They'd dared to harm the woman he loved, and blades or blows, he would see them in hell for that sin.

He glanced over his shoulder to check on her, and when he saw Mellie's blade gleam as she waved it low, one corner of his lips pulled up. "There's my lass."

"Ye're no' sorry I'm no' some refined court lady, who'll go into hysterics and faint?"

His attention was on the danger before him, his sword at the ready, but her sarcastic question had his grin growing ever wider.

He'd thought her as such when he'd first met her, especially when she'd stepped into that alley to defend him, but now?

"I think ye should ken me better than that by now, Mellie."

"Aye," she murmured, "I do."

At that moment, one of the bandits darted forward, and Lachlan easily slapped the man's shorter blade away with his longer sword.

Just who in damnation *were* these men, and why would—

When he recognized the great bull of a man who'd circled in front of him, one meaty fist pounding into the other palm, Lachlan cursed aloud.

'Twas one of the pair of cutpurses who'd tried to rob him —God Almighty, had it been this very square?—the last time he'd been in Scone.

And that meant his wiry little partner had to be here too...*Aye*, there he was.

"Hodan, was it no'?" Lachlan growled, shifting his weight forward. "Or was it Rhys? Did yer master no' say ye were on *watching* duty? Cutting purse strings wasnae lucrative enough for ye, so now ye've turned to attacking innocent ladies?"

"I'm Rhys," the wiry man snarled.

He was the only one of the bandits holding a sword, although he didn't look as if he quite knew what to do with it. Which was unfortunate, because an untrained swordsman is more dangerous than a trained one, Lachlan knew.

Shifting to keep Rhys in front of him, Lachlan felt Mellie turn behind him. They were a good team, in more ways than one.

"My apologies, *Rhys*," Lachlan offered lightly. "Why are ye trying to kill my betrothed?"

Why in damnation hadn't these common thieves run for safety when they saw Mellie was under a warrior's protection?

It was Mellie who answered. "The one whose arm ye took said they were being paid to kill me and make it look like an attack by cutpurses."

That information sent a spike of anger through Lachlan, which he struggled to contain, knowing he'd never manage to keep her safe if he lost control and let emotions take over. He already faced near-impossible odds.

All he allowed himself was a growled, *"Who?"* to Rhys, deciding to treat the wiry man as the leader.

His enemy flicked his gaze over Lachlan's shoulder and gave a subtle nod, just before Mellie sucked in a startled gasp behind him.

Shite!

Taking the risk of leaving himself exposed to Rhys's sword, Lachlan ducked left and twisted his blade under his arm.

Thank the saints he did, because his sword caught Hodan —the giant of a man and Rhys's partner—in the stomach.

Lachlan didn't give himself time to think, but lunged even further left and dragged his blade out through the big man's side.

The weight of his falling enemy almost pulled Lachlan down, but he dropped to one knee and managed to get his sword up in time to block the next attack, which came from two men, who used Hodan's death as a distraction.

Lachlan knew how to fight; he'd been trained and had been in enough battles for the King to know he wouldn't die today, not at the hands of *this* scum.

But he'd never had to fight and worry about the woman he loved either. Each time he twisted out of the way of one blade, he'd lose a precious second or two to glance over at Mellie, ensuring she was still safe.

There were four men in front of him now, which meant the fifth was a direct threat to Mellie, and he couldn't allow that.

Lachlan parried and jabbed, forcing his enemies back, as he did his best to get back to her.

God's Blood, but he couldn't allow her to be hurt!

No matter how unskilled these men were, there were still five additional blades he couldn't juggle.

"Forget the bastard!" one of them panted to another, half in Lachlan's hearing. "Fraser's only paying us to kill the girl, no' the laird!"

Fraser?

Lachlan's surprised hesitation nearly cost him his life.

While his brain tried to make sense of what he'd heard, and still keeping half his attention on Mellie as she sparred with the fifth man, another darted in toward Lachlan's side.

He jerked his blade just in time, slicing into the man's hip.

The enemy went down screaming, but the distraction allowed Rhys to lunge forward, his sword sliding easily into Lachlan's right shoulder.

The pain was immediate and damn near blinding, but Lachlan's hiss was the only indication. He threw himself backward, his flesh sliding from the inexperienced man's blade.

He couldn't allow himself to look, so he shifted his sword's weight to his left hand as the blood pouring out of him made his grip slick.

How could he protect Mellie like this?

Mellie!

Suddenly, she was beside him, her shoulder under his and her arm around his middle. He stumbled sideways, desperate to keep his blade between her and the remaining danger, and caught a glimpse of her opponent from the corner of his eye.

The man was lying on the cobblestones, her blade deep in his throat.

It was useless to them now, and they were down one weapon, but Lachlan couldn't hide his proud grin.

"That's my lass," he whispered again, his voice hoarse from the pain.

"*Sainte Vierge!*" she hissed, her grip around his middle tightening, "What are we to do, Lachlan?"

Without answering her—not altogether sure he *could*—Lachlan began to retreat, trusting her to guide him as well as she could. Together, they stepped back, then back again, but Rhys and his two remaining henchman followed, the gleam of avarice in their eyes.

"What'dya want me to do, Rhys?" one of the other remaining men asked.

"Get around behind them. We don' get paid if the girl don' die, an' now we only have to split the purse three ways!"

Lachlan silently cursed.

Why weren't his legs working properly?

In his condition, he wasn't sure he could fight off even *one* enemy, no matter how untutored the man was. And if one of them got behind them—

Just then, the help they needed came from an unexpected source.

"What purse?"

The growled question—low and angry—came from behind Rhys, who's eyes flicked nervously, but he didn't turn. The man on his right, however, did.

"Shite!" the man groaned.

Lachlan saw their rescuer when the man turned and revealed him; it was the blond stranger, the master of the cutpurses from the alleyway. The one who had no reason to love Lachlan, thanks to the blow he'd given him, which had knocked him unconscious.

But the stranger was holding his sword in the ready position and glaring at Lachlan's attackers.

"Ye nae longer answer to me, Johnnie?" The blond stranger's gaze flicked between the bandits as he stalked closer. "Who paid ye to kill a lass?"

The man, Johnnie, shrugged, his eyes darting to Rhys, then back to the stranger. "One of the Frasers wants her dead, Cam. The auld adviser, Gillepatric. Offerin' to pay us pretty to see it done."

The pain in Lachlan's shoulder was *nothing* compared to the shock of hearing his oldest advisor—his mother's confidante...and mayhap more?—named as the man who'd paid to have Mellie killed.

Is that why Gillepatric had come to Scone?

Had the story about visiting the city with Mother simply been a ploy, an excuse to make contact with this scum for the purposes of—

Nay. Donae think of it.

With the bandits' attention on the newcomer, Lachlan forced himself to just focus on breathing and staying upright.

Ye'll have yer chance soon enough, lad, he promised himself.

Their blond rescuer shook his head and growled at their attackers, "Ye're murderers-for-hire now?"

Johnnie lifted his own blade. "We've always been murderers! *Ye* just thought we could be something different!" he yelled, then lunged toward the man he'd called Cam.

"Nae longer!" Their savior's sword slashed through the air as he parried and attacked. "Ye're nae longer mine!" His sword cut into the cutpurse's neck, and then he turned to Rhys, without even breathing hard.

Lachlan felt his strength draining along with his blood. His sword was too heavy, but he hefted it and attempted to straighten himself, determined not to place too much weight on Mellie.

With one more man down, only Rhys and the other remained. He'd have to kill them before he lost too much blood.

The Fraser battle cry rose up in him.

"I am ready," he whispered, his voice weak, and pushed away from Mellie to stumble forward.

The movement caught Rhys's eye, and the wiry man turned, his sword awkwardly spinning.

"I am ready!" Lachlan repeated, louder and more firmly, and caught the man's blade with his own sword, tossing it to one side, his anger giving his left arm the strength of two men.

And then he heard the cry repeated. "*Je suis prest*! I am ready!"

He thought it came from Mellie's mouth for a brief moment—she was always cursing in her mother's French—but then realized it had been a male voice, and had come from the man named Cam. He glanced left and met the man's gray eyes, only moments before Rhys attacked again.

"*I am ready!*" Lachlan bellowed, just before sinking his sword into Rhys's chest, and watching the man's eyes widen with shock, before glazing over in death.

Although he knew one enemy remained, Lachlan simply couldn't command his arm to pull the blade from Rhys's chest. It seemed all his strength was gone.

He sank to his knees, hearing Mellie scream his name, and knowing he'd failed her.

The stranger—the man she'd once threatened with a knife to his throat, the man who'd admitted to searching for Courtney—had cut down the last of the bandits.

Had one of them really called him *Cam*?

Was it possible this was the man Court considered a brother?

Mayhap there'd be a time when Mellie could ask him, could *think* about asking him, but not now. Not now, as she watched Lachlan's knees give out, then his body crumble to the cobblestones.

She screamed his name and dove toward him, desperate to catch him.

They ended up slumped together in the center of the square, their blades embedded in enemy bodies, and blood and gore all around them. His upper body was sprawled across hers, his head on her shoulder.

"Lachlan?" Her voice quavered as she shook him. *"Lachlan!"*

Blessed Mother of Christ, let him be safe!

There was so much blood, and Mellie could barely breathe as she did her best to turn him over in her arms so she could examine his wound.

Then the stranger—Cam?—was there, helping her.

"No' so mighty now, eh?" he muttered, his hands strong—but gentle—as he lifted and turned Lachlan, resting him back in her arms. "To think someone like ye could damn near break my jaw."

Dimly, through her devastation, Mellie wondered if he was looking for an apology, but the man simply sat back on his heels and exhaled.

"Och," he tsked softly, shaking his head as he prodded at Lachlan's shoulder. "We should get ye to a healer."

"I'll be...aright," came Lachlan's labored response.

He was weak and hurt and had just gone through hell for her, but the sound of his voice was so sweet to hear, Mellie's breath burst out in a relieved sob. "Thank the saints!"

The stranger sank back on his heels. "Ye're a stubborn one, aye?" He still wore the leather trewes and green tunic she'd seen him in all those weeks ago, but now it was blood-spattered. Blood-splatters he'd gained when he'd come to their rescue.

Mellie shook her head, sucking in great gulps of air, as she tried to calm herself. "He *will* be aright, aye. We owe ye thanks, stranger."

The man was still staring down at Lachlan, a frown on his face. "He'll still need a healer."

"I'm taking him to the palace, to the Queen's healer." Mellie lifted her head, searching for someone—*anyone!*—who could help her carry him. "The guards will be here soon enough, I ken it."

The palace was a stone's throw away, after all, and they must've heard the fight.

"The Queen's healer?" The blond man finally met her eyes, one brow raised doubtfully. "For a Fraser?"

He knew of the Crown's recent doubt of the Frasers' loyalty? Mellie found herself bristling, ready to defend the man she loved, but she needn't have bothered.

"No' *a* Fraser, man," Lachlan growled, and when she glanced down at him, he was glaring at the stranger with a fierce curiosity. "*The* Fraser."

If he'd expected humbling, Lachlan would've been surprised.

Instead of apologizing for defaming a Highland laird, for insinuating he wasn't worth the Queen's regard, the blond man went white. Went white, then scrambled to his feet.

"Ye're *Lachlan Fraser?*" he rasped, staring down at them.

Before Lachlan could speak, Mellie tightened her hold on him. "Aye, and what of it? Ye've earned a powerful ally today."

"Lachlan Fraser…?" the man repeated in a mumble, his gray eyes still wide, as he shook his head and stumbled backward. "I cannae… I have t'…"

And then, without another word, he turned and fled.

"*What in damnation?*" Lachlan muttered.

But Mellie pushed all thoughts of their unlikely savior and his odd behavior from her mind and focused on the man in her arms.

"It matters no', my love!"

She shifted her grip, until Lachlan was looking up at her. In the distance, she could hear the shouts of the guards and knew help had finally arrived. Smiling, she tried to ignore the tears freely flowing from her eyes.

"It matters no', because I *will* get ye to the healer, Lachlan. Ye cannae die on me."

Even in his weakened state, Lachlan scoffed, his hand finding her hip. "I willnae die, Mellie. No' now, no' when I've found ye again. Why did ye run?"

Her breath burst out of her on a happy sob. "I love ye, Lachlan Fraser, and I'll explain everything, I swear it."

"Ye love me?"

His voice was sounding weaker, and she tightened her hold on him, willing the guards to arrive faster, so she could get him to the Queen's healer.

"I do! I love ye, Lachlan, and I will keep nae more secrets from ye."

" 'Tis a nice vow," he whispered, his eyes closing, "for I love ye, and I'm dearly tired of no' kenning what the hell is going on."

I love ye.

She was smiling when she lowered her lips to his, her tears splashing against his cheeks.

But he didn't respond, and she knew the vow might've come too late.

CHAPTER 13

He woke to see Mellie's anxious face hovering over him, and Lachlan didn't think he'd ever seen a more beautiful sight.

"Hello, love," he murmured. "Have ye called a healer?"

His shoulder felt as if it was on fire.

Her worried expression eased into a soft smile as she sank down beside him.

Was he on a bed?

Lachlan glanced around, and realized the reason the surroundings looked vaguely familiar, was because he was back in his old chambers in the palace, the one he'd been assigned on his last trip.

"The healer has come and gone, my love," Mellie said in a soft voice, her hand resting on his upper arm. "He stitched ye up easily and says ye're to rest."

Twisting his neck on the pillows, Lachlan followed her gaze to the thick bandage wrapped around his shoulder, then across his chest.

Frowning slightly, he repeated, "Come and gone?" as he

flexed his arm, ignoring the burn from under the bandage, in light of the knowledge his muscles still worked.

"Aye," she said impishly, and when he looked back up at her, a wry grin tugged at her lips. "Ye *fainted*, then slept through the healer's work."

Fainted?

With a growl, Lachlan flexed his injured arm and snagged her around her middle, pulling her atop him. Her fingers splayed across his chest as she landed, and he wasted no time in lifting his chin just enough to give her a hard and fast kiss.

When he dropped his head to the pillows once more, he glared at her. "If ye tell anyone I *fainted*, ye'll get much worse from me, lass."

With a smirk, she patted his bare chest. "I think I'll take my chances, milord."

Chances.

Why did that word cause a sudden tightening in his chest?

What was he afraid of…?

"*Gillepatric!*" Tightening his hold on her, he bolted upright.

His advisor had paid to have Mellie *killed*! As long as the man was still free, Mellie was in danger, and he couldn't take that *chance*.

Against his chest, Mellie exhaled. "He's dead, Lachlan."

What?

Lachlan relaxed his hold just enough, so she was able to push away and look into his eyes, her palm still splayed across his bare skin.

"I donae ken the details, but Gillepatric is dead. When the guards brought ye here, Court met me, and I told her about the threat yer advisor posed. She returned while the healer was working on ye to tell me Gillepatric had been stabbed in his chambers. He was lying across his bed."

Lachlan tried to make sense of her explanation. "Yer friend killed him for ye?"

And why didn't that shock him?

Was it because he was getting used to Mellie's surprises?

Shaking her head, Mellie pushed away and sat up, then began rummaging around for something on the bedside table. "Nay. She prefers her bow. Court said his clothing was askew, as if he had been in the middle of an…an *assignation*, if ye will, and a long dagger was planted into his heart. Court and the guards are searching for his killer now."

Lachlan frowned and allowed himself to fall back against the pillows once more.

Gillepatric was *dead*, paying for his sins…but who had killed him?

And why?

To protect Mellie?

Or for a more sinister reason?

"Why would he have paid to have ye killed?" Lachlan muttered to Mellie's back, as she walked to the other side of the room, then disappearing into a small alcove. "That cutpurse said *ye* were the one they'd been given a purse to see dead."

The thought of what might've happened had he not gotten there in time still made him shudder.

He forced himself to consider all the possible theories he could think of. "Could it be something as simple as Gillepatric didnae approve of my marriage? Or did he no' want me to marry at all? And by all the saints in Heaven, who killed *him*?"

Mellie distracted him from his musings when she moved back into his line of sight, holding a damp cloth and a bowl. Her smile seemed…hesitant almost, as she leaned forward once more and began to wipe his uninjured shoulder and arm.

"I cannae answer these questions, Lachlan. But if we ever find our mysterious savior again, we might be able to ask *him*."

He frowned as he watched her clean the dust of the road from his skin, rinsing the cloth from the bowl of cool water she'd placed on the table beside him. "It sounded as if he didnae ken what—"

When she reached for his neck, he jerked out of the way.

Why in damnation did *bathing* matter now?

"What are ye doing, lass?"

She didn't meet his eyes, but kept them on her hand as she dragged the cool cloth over his forehead and hairline. "Ye're filthy—we're both filthy—and the Queen will be here to see ye soon."

He pushed her hand away and struggled upright once more. "The *Queen*? By His Wounds, why would the *Queen of bloody Scotland* visit me, when I'm looking like this?" He gestured dismissively to his wounded shoulder. "What is going on here, Mellie?"

Taking a deep breath, Mellie stared down at the wet cloth in her hands. "I have a secret, Lachlan. I promised I'd tell ye the truth."

Irritated now, Lachlan snatched the cloth from her hands.

"Aye," he snapped. "Ye also told me ye loved me. Should I doubt that?"

"Never!" Her blue gaze was frantic when she twisted to meet his eyes, her hand reaching for him, almost pleadingly. "*Never*, Lachlan. I love ye, I do. I swear it. I love ye the way I never thought I could love—"

"Aye," he interrupted with a sigh, grabbing her hand and squeezing it. "And I love ye, Melisandre. I'll make ye a deal; I'll wash myself, if ye tell me what I need to ken."

Her eyes jumped between his, her gaze unsure, as if testing for his honesty.

When he winked, she sighed and looked away, but not before he saw the corner of her lips pull up in a slight smile.

"Verra well," she said softly, standing again.

Her back was to him, and she seemed to be staring down at her hands.

"I told ye… I told ye the Queen gave me a place by her side, after my family wanted naught to do with me."

He remembered her tale, the way both her betrothed and her family had made her feel worthless after she lost her bairn, and his fingers squeezed into a fist, causing the cloth to drip water across his lap.

Shaking his head, he forced himself to scrub at the days' worth of road dust which clung to him and focus on her story.

Mellie began to pace, and when he looked up, he saw she was chewing on one fingernail, in that adorable unsure way of hers.

"What I didnae tell ye, *couldnae* tell ye…and mayhap shouldnae even now, although I love ye, and will damn the consequences, nae matter what—"

"Mellie?" he interrupted, hoping to get her back on track, especially if he had a royal visit to prepare for.

With a sigh, she turned to him, the shorter skirts of her traveling gown whirling around her, revealing boots beneath it.

"I am no' just the Queen's lady-in-waiting, Lachlan. I am one of her Angels, one of her *agents*. The three of us—Court, Rosa and I—we are no' just her eyes and ears, but her…*problem solvers*. The missions we undertake are to protect the Crown."

Missions?

Lachlan paused, holding the cloth against the back of his neck and raising a brow at her. *Missions* sounded as if it entailed danger.

Did that mayhap explain the arrow wound in her shoulder, and the other scars he'd seen on her body back at An Torr?

He slowly began to clean his skin again, trying for nonchalance, when he asked, "What do ye do on these missions?"

She shrugged, then lifted her arm to cup the opposite elbow, so she looked as if she were hugging herself. "Courtney was raised by the Red Hand, and I believe the man who rescued us might be the same man she considered a brother. He taught her how to use a bow, how to survive in the wild, so with all that knowledge, it made sense she be our leader."

"When we met in the alleyway, that man told me he was looking for her, did he no'?"

Nodding, Mellie turned back to the window. "Aye, and I donae ken what she will do when I tell her of my suspicions. Rosa now…" She gave a little shake of her head. "Rosalind is a true lady, and more brilliant than anyone I've ever kenned. She reads four languages and can recall most everything she hears. She's the Queen's confidante, the one who can put it all together, when most of us donae see the pattern."

Slowly, Lachlan sat up and placed the cloth back in the bowl, deciding he was clean enough. His skin prickled as the air dried it, but he frowned thoughtfully at the woman he loved. She'd listed her teammate's skills so far, but not her own.

"And ye, Mellie?" he asked quietly.

Her shoulders stiffened, but she did not turn.

"I… I am the whore," she whispered, though she lifted her chin, as if daring him to disapprove. " 'Tis my job to seduce men, to get the information Rosa needs to understand the plots. I am good at—"

With a growl, Lachlan grabbed the coverlet from his legs

and threw it off, swinging his legs off the bed as soon as they were free. "Do no' *ever—*"

In a blink she was beside him, her hands on his shoulders, holding him down on the bed. "Ye cannae walk about yet, Lachlan. Ye'll tear the stitches, and the Queen will be angry."

"And *ye* cannae expect me to sit here, while someone insults the woman I love!" Reaching up, he grabbed her hand from his injured shoulder and pressed his lips to her palm. "Ye are nae whore, Mellie."

She tried to tug her hand away, but he wouldn't let it go. With a sigh, she gave up.

"I *was*, Lachlan," she whispered, staring into his eyes. " 'Twas my job, what I was good at."

"*Nay*. Ye were—ye *are*—good with people, Mellie. Ye understand what motivates them, what they need, what they want. With some men, ye kenned what they wanted was *ye*." And he refused to allow himself to be jealous over that, although the idea of her doubting her worth made him furious.

Her past would *not* affect their future, he vowed.

"But 'tisnae just men, Mellie. I've seen ye with the servants, with my clan, with my *daughter*. With me. Ye *care* about others. *That* is yer talent. Ye care, and ye try to help, and ye give them what they want and need."

During his impassioned speech, her eyes had grown wider. Finally, she sank to the bed beside him, as if her knees had given out.

"Do ye—ye really think that?" she asked him, her whisper full of hesitation.

He pressed another kiss on her palm. "I *ken* it. 'Tis the reason I love ye, Mellie, and I fell in love with ye without yer body being involved. Although…" He had to be honest, so he admitted with a smirk, "ye have a verra fine body indeed."

Her *tsk* sounded irritated at his joke, but he saw the blush crawling up her cheeks, and smiled when she did.

But she snatched the cloth and bowl from the table beside him as she stood, reminding him there was limited time to learn the truth before the Queen arrived.

"Her Majesty betrothed me to ye, no' to secure yer loyalty, as she told ye, but to give me an excuse to investigate ye," Mellie confessed, crossing to a chest on the other side of the room and placing the bowl down. As he watched, she rinsed the cloth out a few times. " 'Twas my job to determine if ye were behind the assassination attempt."

His feet were planted on the floor, his arse still on the bed, but he didn't think he could move as he watched her make short work of unlacing the blue kirtle and slipping it off her shoulders.

"Even *ye* suspected me of something so horrible?" he managed to grind out. He wasn't surprised—there'd been much whispering and distrust in those days following the attack—but it still rankled.

"Aye," she said simply, meeting his eyes as she pulled her braid over one shoulder and reached for the wet cloth. "The assassin called out the name Fraser when he was asked who'd sent him, although Rosa argues he was only acknowledging yer kinsman, Ross, who was present. And the Grants we'd been sent to waylay the night before had all claimed ye—as the new laird—followed in yer father's footsteps as a traitor to the Crown."

Lachlan was having trouble following her words as she dragged the wet cloth down her neck and across her shoulder. His eyes eagerly followed her hand as she tugged the shoulder of her leine out of the way and began to scrub the dark hollow between her breasts. She must've been as road-weary and dirty as he was, but all he wanted to do was pull her back into bed and follow the path of that cloth with his lips.

Focus, lad!

"Grants?" he repeated. Then he frowned, forcing his attention back on her words, and not the way she touched herself as she bathed. "The Grants have been our allies. Why would they claim that?"

She shrugged, then dipped the cloth back in the water once more.

" 'Tis possible they were lying. Rosa later pointed out I may have given them reason to tell me falsehoods. I'd complimented yer looks, ye see, and told them I only had interest in loyal Highlanders."

An inkling of a suspicion rose in Lachlan's mind, and he crossed his arms—ignoring the pull on his wound—and raised a brow at her. "And where were ye when ye made these claims?"

A flush began above her breasts and pinked her neck and cheeks. "In Aboyne. But I suspect ye mean something else. I was on the man's lap," she confessed, without looking at him.

Lachlan's breath burst out of him on a half-laugh, half-groan. "Of *course* the man would tell ye of my guilt, Mellie, if he thought he had a chance with ye! He'd claim the moon was made of *cheese,* if he thought it would make a beautiful woman like ye smile at him."

Her smile was a bit rueful when she finally looked at him. "Aye, 'tis what Rosa said."

Rolling his eyes, Lachlan planted his palms on the mattress once more, bracing his weight. "So yer first two pieces of evidence against me are faulty. Why else did ye think me guilty? Ye nae longer do, aye?"

Her head jerked up and around so fast, her braid swung free of her shoulder. "I *ken* ye are innocent, Lachlan. But when I was sent to An Torr..." With a sigh, she tossed the cloth back into the bowl and began to tug her clothing back into position. "The letter I received had more information in it, and Court filled me in on the rest while the healer worked on ye."

While he was *unconscious*. No' *fainted*.

She held his gaze while she laced herself back up. "Court and Ross went to Kintyre immediately following the assassination attempt, which ye know. There, they found the Red Hand and discovered the group *was* behind the attack. But it wasn't being led by Cam, Court's auld friend. The leader was yer uncle, Andrew Fraser of Lovat."

With a curse, Lachlan shoved himself to his feet, the move sudden enough to cause him to teeter. But he found his balance before she could lunge for him, and held up his hand to stop her.

"Uncle Andrew is *alive*, after all these years?" A thought began nibbling at the back of his mind, but he couldn't concentrate long enough to focus on it, to figure out why Andrew being alive was so important. "And he was behind the assassination?"

Had his uncle inherited his father's seditious beliefs?

When Mellie shrugged, it did interesting things to those big breasts, up until she tucked everything back into her bodice and continued lacing. "Court and Ross killed him, apparently. He claimed the Frasers were behind the attempt because they wanted a Comyn on the throne."

"That's..." He shook his head. "The Red Comyn? The Bruce's only competitor for the throne— He has been dead for years. And his only son died at Bannockburn, did he no'?"

"Aye." Mellie finished, then reached for her braid and untied the end. "So Andrew's claim makes little sense, but 'tis damned incriminating."

His eyes followed her fingers as they ran through her thick golden curls, then deftly began to re-braid them. "To me, ye mean. The Fraser laird."

She nodded briskly. "Ye see why I had to come back, Lachlan?" When he met her gaze, her eyes had a sadness to them. "I had to tell them ye were innocent. *In person*. I *had* to leave."

So she'd left. She'd left to return to Scone, to exonerate *him*.

With another muttered curse, he launched himself forward, stumbling toward the wooden chair placed beside the hearth. He wasn't going to greet the Queen lying in bed, and the way his muscles—and lungs—burned, only served to remind him he was still alive.

And also distracted him from the pain in his heart.

He reached the chair just as Mellie did, and she wrapped her hands around his arm to help him lower himself. But when he was settled and she made to straighten and step away, he grabbed her hand and tugged her into his lap.

And instead of fighting him, she wrapped her arms around his neck.

With his face pressed against her neatly braided hair— how in the hell did she manage to smell so sweet after all those days on the road?—he murmured, "I cannae lose ye, Mellie. Marry me. Be my wife, and a mother to Simone."

But when she stiffened, he knew he'd not get his wish. And the hope he hadn't even realized he'd been harboring, slowly faded from his chest.

"I cannae, Lachlan," she said, as she pushed away from him, meeting his gaze with mere inches separating them. "I'm only betrothed to ye because the Queen commanded it. 'Twas merely a mission."

"Nay!" he snapped, then lowered his voice as he tightened

his hold on her, pulling her heart against his. "*This* is no' merely a mission, Mellie. *We* are no' a mission."

Instead of fighting him—and he was prepared for a fight—she smiled sadly and nodded. "Ye are right. I love ye."

"But?"

"But my place is with the Angels, Lachlan. I made a vow. Nae matter how much I want ye, nae matter how amazed I am that ye could still want me—"

He silenced her with a kiss.

A kiss which showed her *exactly* how much he wanted her, how much he *needed* her.

How much she mattered to him.

And when he pulled away, they were both breathing heavily.

He dropped his forehead to hers. "I've told ye, my angel… I love ye," he whispered. "Ye are the most caring woman I've ever kenned, and I would be lucky to call ye my wife. But…"

She straightened just enough to meet his eyes, her own swimming with unexpected tears. "But what?" she whispered.

"But I understand yer vow," he admitted with a sigh. God help him, but he understood. "I cannae ask ye to give up yer honor to satisfy my desires."

No matter how desperately he wanted a future with her.

When she let out a choked gasp and pressed her lips to his once more—her tears wetting his cheeks, as he captured her sobs with his mouth—he wasn't sure that had been the answer she'd been hoping for.

But what else could he say?

He'd heard her secrets, had accepted them, and knew this was bigger than just the love the two of them had for one another. The Queen—mayhap the entire Crown, even the *nation*!—was in danger, and Mellie had vowed to end the threat.

As a loyal Highlander, Lachlan was duty-bound to help.

But even when this was done, when the Frasers were exonerated, and the guilty party punished, even *then* she would not be free to love him.

And he suspected the tightness in his chest upon realizing that had nothing to do with his wound.

CHAPTER 14

Curled up on Lachlan's lap, Mellie felt as if her heart were breaking.

Even after hearing her confession, hearing the truth of why she'd pretended to be his betrothed, he *still wanted her*. He'd asked her to marry him, not because the Queen had commanded it, but because he *wanted* to be married to her.

And Mellie thought she might choke on her sorrow when she had to say no.

She owed the Queen her loyalty and her service, no matter how badly she yearned to share a future with Lachlan. *And* with Simone.

Dear God, Simone!

Had her bairn lived, she'd be the same age as Simone was now, and it was impossible not to mourn the loss of her child all over again, as she bid goodbye to the possibility of a future as Simone's mother.

'Tis worth it, she reminded herself. It *would* be worth the loss and the pain if, by remaining an Angel, she was able to save Lachlan. If she could convince the Queen he was innocent, she'd not only save his honor, but likely his life.

Her head was tucked under Lachlan's chin, his pulse strong against her lips where they pressed into his neck.

"I am sorry," she whispered against his skin, and when his arms tightened briefly around her, she knew he'd heard her hopelessness.

When the door to the room burst open, Mellie jerked upright, bumping into his chin. Ignoring his quiet curse, she turned, expecting to find the Queen.

But it was Lady Isla Fraser who threw herself into the room with a wail, flying across the chamber to where the two of them were curled together on the chair, much faster than Mellie would've expected.

They ended with the distraught woman atop them as she threw her arms around Lachlan's neck, her wailing and tears making it difficult to understand what she was saying.

Mellie exchanged a surprised—and amused?—glance with Lachlan, before awkwardly extricating herself from between mother and son.

She slid to her feet as Lachlan patted his mother's back, trying to cradle her with his injured arm. The woman didn't seem to notice; she was too intent on her carrying on, her tears soaking his bandages.

"Mother," he began in a soothing voice, and when that didn't get her attention, he tried again, but more firmly. "*Mother*. I am alive and will heal. 'Tis Melisandre who deserves yer fussing. The cutthroats were after her."

"Nay!" Isla wailed, tightening her hold on his neck, as if afraid he would pull her away. "Ye are my son, my boy! Naught is ever supposed to happen to ye, no' while I live! And ye were wounded!" she ended, with a howling sob.

Still patting her back awkwardly, Lachlan met Mellie's eyes over his mother's head, and raised a brow, as if to ask what he should do. Mellie's lips twitched, before she managed to school her features into a mask of concern.

Clearly the poor woman was near delusional with fear. Had she heard what had happened to her dear friend Gillepatric? Mayhap that news was what had set her over the edge.

"Come, milady," she said gently, reaching for the older woman. She wrapped her arm around Isla's shoulders and tugged her away from Lachlan, but the woman refused to let go of her son. "Let me help ye here to this bench, Isla."

Eventually, Mellie managed to move the older woman to the bench opposite the chair, but Lachlan had to go with them, because Isla's hold on him was tight. The two of them ended up beside one another, with his uninjured hand in both of his mother's, and her head on his shoulder as she cried quietly.

"I'm so sorry, my lad," she kept repeating, as Lachlan did his best to comfort her. " 'Tis a horrible thing to happen, so scary!"

"Mother," Lachlan tried again, "I will be well. The attack was no' meant for me, but—"

"Attack!" the woman interrupted with another wail, "Oh, by all the saints in Heaven, nay!" And she dissolved into another bout of weeping.

God forgive her, but Mellie was almost relieved when the door opened once more and Liam Bruce stepped into the room.

The Queen's bodyguard was still strong and intimidating, despite the gray at his temples, and he settled against the wall with his hand on the hilt of his sword, then nodded to someone in the hall.

Queen Elizabeth swept into the room, looking as regal as ever, followed closely by Rosa. When she saw her dear friend, Mellie couldn't help the whimper of joy which burst from her lips, and the two flew across the room to embrace.

Rosa's dark hair was pulled back in braids, and she was

slight enough that Mellie near enveloped her when she hugged her friend again. But as usual, the younger woman's reserve wasn't evident around her fellow Angel.

"I've missed ye so, Mellie," she whispered against Mellie's shoulder. "I've been so worried for ye!"

Mellie tugged her toward the hearth, so they'd have a bit of privacy. "Lachlan saved me, Rosa! He was magnificent, ye should've seen him! He came riding into the square like some sort of—"

"No' today," Rosa scolded quietly, "I only just found out about the attack. I meant the last fortnight, kenning naught of yer situation at An Torr and what ye'd found."

The reprimand sobered Mellie, and when Rosa took her hands, she had trouble meeting her friend's eyes. "I am sorry, Rosa. I…I wasnae sure what to write, at first…"

Her friend squeezed her hands. "And now, dear one?"

"I…ken the truth."

Rosa nodded to the Queen, who was watching the two of them. "Then speak it, Mellie. *Dicere verum.*"

Half the time, Mellie had no idea what the Latin phrases her friend sometimes spouted meant, but this one was clear. *Speak the truth?* Aye, she would.

Lifting her head, she met the Queen's gaze and took a deep breath.

But before she could speak, one of Elizabeth's hands raised imperiously to halt her. "Courtney has shared with us both the details of the attack, as you shared them with her. Most importantly, that Gillepatric Fraser paid cutpurses to kill you, but is in fact now dead himself."

When Mellie nodded, albeit hesitantly, the Queen's gaze flicked to Lachlan, who was now watching them over his mother's head, although Mellie wasn't sure if he could hear what was being said.

"We can assume Gillepatric Fraser was working under

orders from someone else. Someone who has since murdered him," Elizabeth stated.

And Mellie understood what she was saying.

Taking a deep breath, Mellie knew everything—Lachlan's very life!—rested on her next words.

"No' Laird Lachlan Fraser, Yer Majesty."

When Elizabeth turned to her, one regal brow raised, Mellie reached for the Queen's—her *friend's*—hands. "Lachlan is innocent, Elizabeth. I swear it on my own life." She squeezed the other woman's hands in emphasis. "He is a *good* man."

Elizabeth's sharp eyes bore into Mellie's. "Do you know of another suspect? Before his death, Andrew Fraser claimed the Frasers of Lovat were behind the assassination. And a Fraser advisor has been implicated in this last attack. It would make sense to lay the blame at the feet of the Fraser laird."

"Aye, 'twould," Mellie reluctantly agreed. "But only if that man were no' Lachlan. I *ken* he is a good man, a loyal Scottish subject, who values his fealty to ye and King Robert. He would *never* give orders which would threaten that relationship, and thus his clan's future. He's a warrior, aye, but he values peace."

Queen Elizabeth eyed her for a long moment, then dropped her gaze to their clasped hands. "Do you love him?"

Mellie's response was immediate and certain. "I do. With all my heart. I never kenned 'twas possible to feel this way about a *man*."

Although her gaze didn't lift, the Queen's lips twitched, mayhap in response to Mellie's emphasis. It was known Elizabeth valued her friendships with her ladies—especially her Angels—as strongly as her relationship with her husband. And after five years of working with Charlotte, Court and Rosa, Mellie felt the same way.

"High praise, indeed," Elizabeth murmured, then settled into silence as she considered.

In the stillness, Isla Fraser's sniffling seemed even louder, but Mellie couldn't drag her gaze away from the Queen's thoughtful expression, and she prayed for Lachlan's future.

Rosa moved to stand beside Mellie, her light touch on her arm offering much-needed support.

Finally, Elizabeth sighed and lifted her eyes to Mellie's. "Is it possible Gillepatric was acting alone? That mayhap he was behind both attacks?"

Relief slammed into Mellie so quickly, her knees went weak. It was only her hold on the Queen's hands, and Rosa's touch on her elbow, which kept her upright.

Queen Elizabeth believed her!

She believed that Lachlan was innocent!

Sainte Vierge, he would be safe!

She closed her eyes on a prayer of thanks, as Rosa hummed in consideration.

" 'Tis possible, Yer Majesty, but I am doubtful. It seems too convenient, considering he is now dead. Would he act thusly without orders?" Rosa asked.

Mellie's head jerked up. "Lachlan didnae order it; I *ken* that much."

"Someone else then?" Rosa murmured, her touch on Mellie's arm dropping away, as she tilted her head back to stare up at the ceiling, the way she always did when she was deep in thought. "Andrew, mayhap? He was the auld laird's brother, and likely had sway among the Frasers. Court's account of his death does no' actually preclude his leadership of the entire scheme."

Mellie exchanged glances with the Queen, and hated the hopeful look in Elizabeth's eyes. Wincing, Mellie shrugged. "I cannae say, Rosa. I ken Andrew has been away from the Frasers for many years. He left nigh fifteen years ago, following his youngest nephew, who had left home for...*personal* reasons."

"Cameron," Rosa acknowledged with another murmur, her mind clearly whirling behind her dark eyes. "If Andrew has no' been home in that time, then 'tis unlikely he's had much contact with Gillepatric."

"We cannae ken that for certain," Mellie interrupted, grasping desperately for logic. " 'Tis possible Andrew concocted the entire scheme from wherever he's been hiding. The Red Hand were responsible, after all, and Andrew—"

As she said the man's name again, another wail rose behind her, and all three women turned to see Isla throw herself against her son's chest once more, her fist pounding his uninjured shoulder as she howled about her dear brother-in-law's murder.

Mellie met Lachlan's eyes, his clear gray orbs showing only worry for his mother.

Had she heard the rumors of Andrew's death since her arrival in Scone?

The poor woman!

To first learn of her brother-in-law's death, then have her son attacked and injured, *and then* to also lose a dear friend and advisor, all in one day...

'Twas no wonder her mind was somewhat broken.

Mellie's heart swelled with pity, and she would've gone to help Lachlan with his mother, but she could not abandon the Queen right in the middle of a conversation.

She begged him with her eyes to understand, and the little nod he gave her over his mother's head told her he did.

Everyone's attention was caught when Liam stepped away from the wall, as he half-drew his sword from the scabbard at his hip.

Elizabeth stiffened, just as Mellie heard the sound of

running feet in the hall. Court burst into the room, her wild expression immediately transforming into relief once she saw everyone was together, and for the most part, alive and well.

At the sight of her, both Liam and the Queen relaxed with a sigh.

Court stalked across the room and gathered both Mellie and Rosa in her strong embrace. Before Mellie even had a chance to return the hug, Court had already stepped back and sent a brisk nod in the Queen's direction.

"Nae sign of the murderer; Ross is still leading the search. We'll find the bastard who did this." She scowled. "Took plenty of bollocks to murder a man right here in the palace, nae matter he was doing us a favor."

Her lips twitching at the vulgarity Court was obviously too agitated to realize she'd used, Queen Elizabeth nodded. "As Rosalind pointed out, it's certainly very convenient."

Court's glance at Lachlan was telling, and Mellie hurried to defend the man she loved. "Lachlan didnae give the orders, nor did he kill Gillepatric, Court. The Queen believes in his innocence."

The tall woman turned an incredulous expression toward Mellie, so Rosa leaned forward, and in that calm way she had of keeping her team connected, said simply, "She loves him."

Court's countenance shifted to confusion, and then to Mellie's surprise, she flushed.

Mayhap this warlike Angel really *had* found love with Ross Fraser!

Before Mellie could question her, Court rolled her eyes and huffed.

"So no' the laird. Fine. Who else?"

Before they could re-hash their non-existent list of suspects once more, Rosa spoke up, saying, "Tell us of yer mysterious savior, Mellie."

When Mellie turned, her brows drawn in confusion, Rosa clarified.

"In yer initial report, ye said another man stepped up to help defeat the cutpurses this afternoon."

"Aye." With a brisk nod, Mellie made short work of describing the battle, and the blond man who'd appeared in time to save them. She finished with, "And 'tis no' the first time we've seen him. Ye recall our confrontation in the alleyway before I left Scone?"

The three Angels—and the Queen—were grouped together now, their heads bent. Court was frowning, of course, but Rosa nodded.

"Aye, I filled Courtney in when she returned."

"Including the part about him asking after her?"

Court hissed. "Nay, she left that part out."

Under her dark skin, Rosa flushed, but met her friend's eyes defiantly. "I didnae want to worry ye, no' until Mellie returned."

"*Rosalind*," Court growled in warning.

Mellie was the one to lift her hands in peace. "The man was the leader of the cutpurses who were trying to steal from Lachlan—two men who were among the attackers today, I might add. All three of them admitted to being members of the Red Hand, although the stranger indicated they were nae longer supposed to be thieving." She swallowed and met Court's eyes. "He said he was looking for ye. He said he'd tracked ye as far as Scone Palace, but couldnae get inside."

In the years they'd worked together, the three of them had garnered more than a few enemies, but none of them had caused the sort of fear which now leeched Court's face of color.

Blindly, she reached out for support, and her friends were there to grab her arms and hands and lower her onto a stool.

Once seated, Court didn't release Mellie's hand, but

instead, gripped it even tighter. "Tell me," she commanded in a hoarse whisper. "Tell me what he looked like."

Mellie sunk to her knees beside her friend, knowing of the fierce hope and fear which must be warring against each other in Court's heart. She knew what her fellow Angels suspected.

"He was tall and somehow familiar. Blond hair, rather on the longish side. Well-built, and he carried himself regally, though he was dressed in simple clothes and wore nae clan colors."

Court's stare drilled desperately into hers. "Gray eyes?"

When Mellie nodded solemnly, Court let out a noise much like a groan as she doubled over. "Cam! Oh, Blessed Virgin, *Cam*!"

Mellie extricated her hand from Court's grip to reach around her shoulders, attempting to hold her up the same way she'd held the still-weeping Isla a short time before.

But she should've known better. Her friend was stronger than her grief.

When Court suddenly straightened, it wasn't tears in her eyes, but determination, as she twisted to find Mellie. "Cam sent me away to save me, and now he's looking for me. Before we killed him, Andrew said Cam had left the Red Hand to find me, but I never, *ever* thought he'd discover where I was." She took a deep breath. "I have to find him. When all this is done, I have to find him again."

Knowing how much the man meant to her, knowing how he'd all but raised Court, and that she considered him a brother, Mellie squeezed her friend's shoulders.

Cam's betrayal had almost broken Court all those years ago, but if she'd discovered new information—he'd sent her away to *save* her?—it might explain her new feelings for Ross.

Mellie glanced over at Lachlan, where his head was bent over his mother's as he spoke soothingly to her, and remembered how she'd thought he'd known the stranger when she'd first seen them in the alley.

But despite their similar builds and eye color, Lachlan had been surprised to see the stranger again.

But the stranger...?

Remembering the man—Cam's—reaction this afternoon, Mellie slowly pushed herself to her feet, her hand still on Court's shoulder, and met Rosa's eyes.

"Today, Cam recognized the Fraser plaid. When he learned Lachlan was the laird, he kenned his name."

Court grunted. "He was always good at reconnaissance. Likely, he'd just learned the Fraser's given name."

Mellie shook her head, trying to grasp *why* the man's reaction had been so strange. "When he discovered who Lachlan was, he acted as if he'd been burned, so quickly did he leave. As if he'd seen a ghost almost."

As Mellie had known it would, this new piece in their twisted and confusing puzzle caught Rosa's attention. She hummed thoughtfully and tilted her head back.

"Cam..." the youngest Angel whispered. "Cameron? Is it possible...?" She took a deep breath and turned her attention to the pair sitting on the bench at the other side of the room. "Is it possible Courtney's Cam is really *Cameron Fraser*? The missing son? The one whom Andrew Fraser followed all those years before?"

A feeling of certainty began to build within Mellie.

She helped Court stand, but maintained her hold on her friend.

"Cameron Fraser," Mellie repeated in a low voice.

Court nodded thoughtfully. "He was always nobler than all of us put together, although he did his best to forget it and learn the thieves' code. I remember the other lads teasing him, calling him *laird*, until he grew big enough to beat them all, and they finally stopped."

Rosa was still staring at Isla Fraser, who had lifted her head to stare back. "She'll have to be told, Court. Yer past with him needs addressing, but she's his *mother*. If Cameron Fraser still lives, she must ken it."

Before any of them could respond, the older woman's tear-stained face broke into a wide grin, and a crazed laugh burst from her lips.

CHAPTER 15

God's Wounds!
His mother's moods would never cease to confuse him!

Her madness had begun close to fifteen years ago, after her youngest son's disappearance.

She'd been difficult since then, but *this...*?

This was something new.

Her clinginess, the hysteria...he'd never seen her this bad before.

And when his mother threw back her head and burst into great, heaving laughs, he knew her mind had officially, and likely irreversibly, broken.

Holding her upright, despite the pain in his shoulder, Lachlan's gaze sought out Mellie's, and was surprised to see her staring at his mother with something akin to fear in her expression.

Why would a woman—who'd killed a man today to save their lives—be so afraid of Isla Fraser's madness?

Unless something *else* had her worried.

"Cameron!" His mother's laughter had subsided into odd

hiccuping sobs. "My Cameron!" she cried with a smile, even as tears rolled down her cheeks.

When she threw herself against Lachlan's chest again, he realized she was calling *him* Cameron and closed his eyes on a brief prayer.

God in Heaven, have mercy on her!

Losing her youngest son had been bad enough—all the saints knew Lachlan himself had taken years to recover from that loss—but to only just discover Andrew's death must've been like losing them both all over again.

And the attack on Lachlan, the same day of Gillepatric's murder, must have simply been too much for her to comprehend.

And now she thought *he* was his dead brother.

"Cameron, I *kenned* ye'd come back to me!" She was patting his cheek as she rocked against him. "After all I've done for ye, I *kenned* ye werenae dead! Yer uncle kept ye safe all these years, my lad, did he no'?"

To his surprise, it was the dark-skinned lady, one of Mellie's friends, who pulled his mother away, wrapping her arms around the older woman's shoulders and helping Isla to her feet.

"Come, Lady Fraser," she murmured, offering Lachlan a reassuring smile, "let me help ye to yer chambers. I have much to tell ye, now that ye ken yer Cameron lives."

Frowning, Lachlan watched them shuffle out of the room, the younger woman all but holding up his hysterical mother.

Why would the lady claim Cameron was still alive?

Was she simply wise to what would calm his broken mother and allow her to get some much needed rest?

Lachlan cursed his daft wound and the subsequent weakness for preventing him from going after the pair, his protective instincts still on high alert. But when he met Mellie's eyes and saw the worry in them, he knew he couldn't leave her when she looked at him that way.

As soon as his mother stepped out of the room, those remaining seemed to exhale as one.

Mellie exchanged a glance with the tall woman beside her, then hurried to his side. Not that he was complaining—he grabbed her hand and pulled her down to the bench beside him as soon as she was close enough—but he hated not understanding events going on around him.

"What is it, love?" he asked gently, before she was even fully seated.

When she lifted her fingernail to her lips, he then knew she *was* nervous about whatever was going on, and mayhap even nervous to tell him what it was.

So he squeezed her hand. "*Mellie,*" he growled. "Tell me."

At his command, she sighed and dropped her hand. "Cameron. *Cam.* It's him."

She was making about as much sense as his mother..

He frowned.

Cam...?

The name tickled something in the back of his mind, something he couldn't quite grasp.

Cam...?

Cameron?

Had anyone ever called his brother Cam?

But something must've shown in his expression, because Mellie was nodding. He lifted his head to suck in some much needed air, and was startled to find the others gathered in a semi-circle in front of them.

Mellie gave his hand a light squeeze, then said, "Courtney was raised by the Red Hand, Lachlan. The man she knew as her brother, the man who ran the criminal organization, was named Cam. He's the one who ye met in the alleyway, all those weeks ago. And the one who saved us today."

Flashes of memories lit the space behind Lachlan's lids: the stranger's tight frown; his familiar gray eyes; the easy smile when he'd mentioned Lachlan's punch.

The look of terror on his face when he'd realized Lachlan's name.

"He's yer brother, Lachlan," Mellie whispered, sorrow in her expression. "Cameron is alive."

Recognition slammed into him, and he knew she was right.

"Cameron's alive?" he whispered, his eyes going wide as more memories threatened to overwhelm him. Memories of a boyhood twenty years past, of laughter and pranks and pain he'd thought long buried. And fifteen long years of sorrow. "All this time…?"

My little brother is alive?

The churning in his stomach—part guilt, part joy—worked its way up his throat, and he wasn't sure if he was elated or nervous about this new revelation.

But why was Mellie still looking at him with such sadness in her lovely blue eyes?

Because he's the one behind this plot, ye clot-heid!

"Cameron has been running the Red Hand, and Uncle Andrew was with him," he stated, lifting his gaze to hers, then glancing at the Queen. "All of yer evidence points to a Fraser behind the treason, and I ken naught of it." He met Mellie's eyes once more. "Ye think Cameron is guilty? Even though he saved our lives today?"

"He saved our lives, before he kenned who we were," she reminded him gently.

God's Wounds, all the hints!

All the familiarity and the similarities and—

Lachlan cursed, remembering how he'd *known* the stranger's fighting moves, before he'd even made them.

Because the same man taught us both: Uncle Andrew.

The Queen folded her hands in front of her. "Am I to understand we have identified the guilty Fraser?"

The bodyguard—the one who hadn't spoken a single word, up 'til now—cleared his throat. "The Angels' investigation has laid the fault on the Frasers' of Lovat. I kenned Ross was innocent of the suspicion, but if ye've determined the laird is as well"—he nodded to Lachlan—"then the laird's younger brother, who led the Red Hand for years, and who Andrew Fraser would ken well, is our only remaining suspect."

Queen Elizabeth was frowning thoughtfully as she addressed Lachlan. "And what would his motivation be?"

Helpless, Lachlan shook his head. "I— I donae ken, Yer Majesty. Our father had nae love for yer husband, but Cameron ran off long before Robert was ever made king. Why would he harbor our da's hatred throughout these last fifteen years and do naught 'til now?"

Mellie swung her head towards her tall friend. "Court, ye said Andrew of Lovat had been at Cam's side all these years, aye?"

The woman—Court—tapped her bow against her thigh as she nodded curtly. " 'Tis possible that the man soured Cam's mind in the years since I've seen him, but—"

"Mayhap he wants the lairdship," Liam interrupted. When Court turned to frown at him, he shrugged, his hand resting easy on the hilt of his sword. "Nae one kenned he was even alive. Mayhap his intention was to lay the blame at Lachlan's feet, then take over the clan after the execution?"

Lachlan's eyes narrowed, his throat constricting at the thought of a traitor's death, despite his certainty that Mellie believed his innocence.

The Queen hummed. " 'Tis an elaborate scheme, and a dangerous one. Court, would Cam—the man ye ken as a brother—order my death?"

Court's response was a pause, then a reluctant shrug. "I cannae say, Yer Majesty. The man I kenned wouldnae, for all that he was a thief. But he sent me away seven years ago. 'Tis been long enough for him to change, I suppose."

"Long enough to turn into this degree of evil?" Mellie asked skeptically.

When Court shrugged, Lachlan caught Mellie's gaze, and knew she was thinking the same thing he was. The man who'd saved them today, the man who'd chuckled easily about Lachlan's punch, the man who'd seemed anguished as he looked for Courtney in the alleyway…hadn't *seemed* evil.

How could a man order his monarch's death, yet save two strangers' lives?

How could my brother *do such a thing?*

To Lachlan's surprise, the Queen took one of Court's hands in her own, and her voice was gentle when she said, "I understand, dear Courtney. You've only just forgiven him for his actions, thanks to what you learned on your recent mission. And to discover him a traitor so soon after…"

The tall woman—who looked so much like a warrior—seemed to melt under the Queen's regard. Court stared down at their joined hands, but her voice was hard, when she muttered, "I'll ask him when I find him," and it sounded much more like a threat, than a promise.

The bodyguard glanced at the door, just a moment before the dark-haired Angel slipped back into the room and sent a small nod to Lachlan, letting him know his mother was safe in her chambers with her maids.

"Excellent timing, Rosa," the Queen complimented, as Court straightened and pulled her hand back. "We were just discussing my Angels' next mission."

"Finding Cam," Court confirmed in a cold voice. "Not to thank him, but to discover the truth."

"Ye think he's the one who killed Gillepatric?" Rosa asked.

Court expression remained hard and unforgiving. "He's our only viable suspect for the whole damnable plot."

Suspect.

Not so long ago, Lachlan had been in that same position. And now…?

Now, he was going to lose Mellie.

The Queen of Scotland had just given Mellie a mission—a mission to track down his own treasonous younger brother—and he knew the Queen's orders were more important than any vows of love he may share with Mellie.

Mayhap Mellie guessed the same, because without looking at him, her hand tightened around his.

"But…"

At the warning in the Queen's voice, he dragged his attention away from his love.

"You will not be going, Melisandre."

Slowly, Mellie stood, her hand slipping out of his grip. "Yer Majesty?"

"Court and Rosalind will be tasked with hunting down this Cameron Fraser and obtaining the needed answers. *You*, my dear, will have your own mission."

Was this going to be better or worse than knowing she'd be tasked with locating his brother to answer for his crimes?

The band squeezing around Lachlan's chest made it difficult to breath.

Or mayhap it was only his fresh wound.

"What would ye have me do?" Mellie straightened her shoulders, but Lachlan could hear the pain in her voice when she stood before the Queen. "I owe ye my vow, and my verra life, Elizabeth. Say what ye need, and I'll follow yer command without question."

The Queen stepped forward and lifted her hand, then placed it on Mellie's shoulder in a sort of benediction. "Your mission, as Lady Fraser, will be to secure peace in Lovat," she said in a gentle voice. "There is treachery afoot, and I trust you absolutely, my dear. You will ensure none of that treachery spills over to Lovat, and you will ensure your people and clan are allowed to live in peace."

The Queen then dropped her hand and stepped back. The silence, which spread through the small room, stretched for a dozen heartbeats, then a dozen more, as Lachlan held his breath, waiting for Mellie to answer.

Waiting for her to understand what their Queen had just commanded.

Finally, her voice quavering, she whispered, "Lady Fraser?"

Lachlan wasted no further time.

Ignoring the pull of his stitches and the ache in his arm, Lachlan pushed himself to his feet, then reached for Mellie. He lifted his uninjured arm to cup the side of her face, while resting his other on one of her curvaceous hips.

"That's *twice* now ye've been ordered to marry me, Mellie. So what say ye finally follow through, eh?" He held his breath as he waited to hear her answer.

And to his immense relief, her lips twitched upward, even though her eyes showed her sincerity. "Well, I have *always* been a loyal Angel."

When the Queen cleared her throat, they both glanced at her, but Lachlan couldn't make himself ease his hold on the woman he loved, and Mellie didn't seem anxious to leave his hold any time soon either.

"A love as strong and certain as what you have found is a rare and special thing, Lady Melisandre Lamond," Elizabeth stated regally. "I relieve you of your vows to me and wish you all the peace and joy in your future with your husband."

They had their Queen's blessing!

Without acknowledging his monarch, and without giving Mellie time to as well, he turned her head back to his and captured her lips in a kiss designed to show her just how much she meant to him.

How much he loved her.

How much he needed her at An Torr.

How much he intended to treasure her, to worship her, for the rest of their lives.

How much he *needed* a future with her as his wife and mother to his daughter.

The kiss sent him reeling.

With a gasp, he pulled away and pressed his forehead to hers. Both were still as they gulped for air.

He wasn't sure what *she* was thinking, but he was desperately trying to keep his cock under control.

The bloody Queen of Scotland is standing right over there, ye clot-heid!

Finally, he eased his hold on her and swallowed. "Marry me, lass. Be my wife."

She pulled away, but only far enough to gaze into his eyes.

And when her lips broke into a smile, he thought he might've died and gone to Heaven.

"Aye, Lachlan! But I'll want more bairns."

Just like that, the fist squeezing his heart eased, and he could breathe once more. But before he could kiss her again, before he could even control the smile which threatened to split his face in two, her friend Rosa huffed.

"I suppose I'll have to teach her how to *count* again, but for the opposite result," she whispered loudly.

Bursting into laughter, Mellie pulled away from him, but wrapped her arm around his middle even as she reached out her other hand to her friend. All the women were chuckling, which told Lachlan it was a joke between them, even if he didn't understand it.

And at that moment, he didn't care. He was getting everything he'd wanted: Mellie would be his wife, and the Frasers would finally have peace.

Thoughts of Cameron—his brother was alive!—threatened his newfound happiness, but he pushed them down. Right now, he held the woman he loved and had just been promised a future with her.

That was enough.

Mellie was still smiling as she said to the Queen, "I owe ye so much, Yer Majesty. And now even more! I hope ye'll consent to a royal visit to An Torr sometime? The waters of Loch Ness are stunning, if ye avoid the summer storms, and ye have to hear the stories of the monster who lives there! Oh, and Rosa!" She reached for her friend. "I cannae *wait* to introduce ye to wee Simone. She's so smart, ye'll love her right away."

Rosa patted her hand. "I look forward to meeting yer daughter," she said with a gentle smile.

"Daughter…" Mellie breathed reverently, then turned a bright smile to Lachlan. "I'll be her mother, will I no'?"

His hold on her tightened, and he resisted the urge to burrow his face in her sweet-smelling curls. "Ye'll be the best mother she could hope for, love."

The Queen interrupted them again when she cleared her throat. "I would be pleased to see you married here in Scone, if you can delay your return to An Torr. And although you have your new mission, I would appreciate your insights into this current dilemma."

Dilemma?

What a simple way to call something so complex!

But Mellie nodded eagerly as she glanced his way. "I cannae imagine Lachlan wanting to leave without answers about his brother. Are ye willing to stay a bit longer?"

Stay in Scone?

He remembered the way his head had ached the last time

he'd been here, the way all the simpering and bowing and *politeness* had grated on his nerves, when he'd much rather have been at home, improving An Torr or hunting for his people, or even out on the loch with his daughter.

But gathered in this room were the very people who would've given him that headache, but now he realized they were *friends*. And he didn't have to avoid them, or yearn for his home any longer. If Mellie was here with him and willing to introduce him to *her* life, he'd be happy to stay here a bit longer.

As long as he could take her back to An Torr when this was all over.

So he nodded. "If I can send an escort for Simone, with instructions for Owen and Marcus in my absence, I'd be pleased to marry ye here, and stay as long as the Queen would have us."

After all, his mother was already in Scone, and Simone was the only other family he'd insist on having at his wedding.

Briefly, his mind jumped to his treasonous younger brother, back from the dead, but he pushed thoughts of Cameron away. *He* couldn't count as family anymore—not if he was a traitor—for all that Lachlan owed Cameron his life.

Rosa clapped her hands eagerly, her smile genuine. "Mellie and Court have both found love! I cannae believe how much things will be changing."

Court elbowed the younger woman. "We need to find *ye* a man now," she announced, in that gruff way of hers.

Mellie giggled as Rosa flushed.

"Nay, thank ye. I am happy here at Elizabeth's side. She'll need me more than ever, once Mellie is gone."

Court rested her palms atop her bow, the back of one hand revealing a distinctive thief's brand. "Ye'll have me and Ross. Between the three of us, we'll keep the Queen safe."

"And what about me and my men?" the bodyguard rumbled from his place against the wall. "Are we worth so little?"

All of them chuckled, and Mellie waggled her finger at him. "Now that ye're a father, Liam, yer attention will be divided. When can I meet wee Roger?"

Liam grinned proudly. "I'm surprised Charlotte isn't in here with the lad already. Ye'll have to visit her as soon as ye can, or she'll have my hide. But"—he leveled a mock glare at Mellie—"don' give in to her demands for a report. She *has* to rest, and ye are no' one of her Angels anymore."

The reminder sobered Mellie, and her eyes turned sad as she looked back at her friends. "I'll miss ye more than ye'll ken."

But it was the Queen who scoffed and tsked disapprovingly at her bodyguard, before turning her full attention to Mellie. "Being an Angel is not something you just give up, Melisandre. You will be married, you will have a new role, but you will *forever* be one of my Angels!"

"I—" Mellie's voice cracked, and she shook her head, then smiled softly. "I love ye all."

Gently, Lachlan turned her to him, and her smile grew.

"And *ye*, Laird Fraser…I love ye more than I thought possible."

He was grinning as he leaned toward her. "And I love ye, my Angel."

His lips closed on hers, and the vow became reality.

There, in her arms, he found his promise of forever.

EPILOGUE

"Come here, *wife*."

At Lachlan's growled command, Mellie didn't bother hiding her joy. And when he saw her smile, her husband mirrored it, just before pulling her hips flush against his and lowering his lips to the smooth skin of her neck.

Husband!

The word would never cease to amaze her, even once the newness wore off.

She was *married*, as of this morning, and still felt a little dazed over it.

But her husband's lips were being sufficiently distracting.

With a gasp, she flexed her pelvis, grinding herself against his stiffening member.

"Lachlan!" she moaned, allowing her head to fall back so his lips could trail down toward her breasts. "Please!"

"Aye, *wife*," he murmured against her skin, and she could hear the grin in his voice.

It seemed he was just as enamored with their new status as she was.

When he kicked the door to his chambers closed, it was easy to forget the wedding feast and friends who had teased them with knowing looks. It was easy to allow her world to shrink to this room, this *bed*, and what her love was doing to her.

And what she could do to him.

Over the last three weeks, much had changed. Simone had settled in at Scone for a long visit, and they'd gotten to the bottom of the twisted, treasonous plot against the Crown.

But one thing which *hadn't* changed, was her feelings for this man.

Each night, after his shoulder had healed enough, he'd visited her in her small chambers, and they'd spoken of the future they would build together, as their naked limbs twined around one another.

She'd had three weeks to learn what her husband liked, and fully intended to employ the entirety of her knowledge tonight.

His hand was already reaching for her breast—one of those things she'd learned he liked very much—when she stepped back and sank to her knees in front of him.

"Mellie—"

"Shh," she cautioned him, reaching for his kilt. "Let me."

He made a strangled sort of noise as she lifted the Fraser plaid, revealing the hard and swollen length of him. But when she cupped his bollocks and lowered her lips, he jerked away.

"Mellie, ye don' have to…"

From her spot on the floor before him, she met his eyes, remembering the time she'd lowered herself in this same way previously. He'd had the strength to deny her then, but the liquid heat in his beautiful gray eyes *now,* told her he was ready this time.

Then, she'd made this offer only to manipulate and seduce him.

Now, she did it out of love.

"Please, Lachlan," she whispered, letting all the love she felt seep into her voice. "Let me do this for ye."

A groan marked his surrender, as his hand dropped to her hair, and his head fell back.

Sainte Vierge, but he was so very large!

It wasn't the first time she'd tasted a man's cock, but it was the first time it made her feel so *powerful*. The noises he made, the way his skin flexed beneath her ministrations, made her wet and desperate in a way she'd never experienced.

Her fingers inched her skirts up as she knelt on the floor, the fabric skimming over her sensitive skin. When she touched her own dampness, she surged forward with a moan, taking him farther down her throat.

That was the limit for him, and Lachlan broke away with a growl, then reached down and pulled her into his arms in one movement.

Before she knew it, she was on the bed, her skirts bunched around her hips, and he was plunging into her.

"God Almighty," he groaned, resting his forehead against her shoulder, as he gulped in big breaths of air. "I wanted to go slow tonight and savor my wife."

Under him, she wriggled slightly, not bothering to hide her smile as the pressure built in all the right places.

He pulled back to look into her eyes. "I'm sorry, wife, but—"

"Take me, Lachlan," she commanded. "We can go slow next time."

With a groan of surrender, Lachlan anchored her hips to his and rolled over, taking her with him. They were both still clothed, both panting and desperate, both tangled in the coverlet and her skirts.

It was *perfect*.

She loved when he allowed her to be in the position of power like this, with the ability to set the pace and the pressure. She loved feeling in control and loved the way it aroused her. When his tempo changed, she knew he was ready to lose himself inside her, so she leaned forward and planted her hands on either side of his head.

Lachlan could apparently tell she was close to her own fulfillment, because his palms grasped her arse cheeks, and his fingertips brushed against her secret pleasure spot, causing her to scream his name as she climaxed.

Thoroughly spent, she collapsed onto Lachlan's chest, and they were quickly lost in a jumble of clothing, both a hot and tangled mess. They were chuckling when she finally pushed herself upright and rolled off him.

"That was…" Unable to find the words to express how amazing their lovemaking was, Mellie trailed off with a sigh.

Pushing himself up on one elbow, Lachlan's grin showed how proud of himself he was. "If *that's* what married life is like, I'll gladly take it." His hand drifted to the curves of her stomach. "And ye'll have that bairn ye want before long, because I plan on exercising my husbandly duty as often as possible."

Mayhap it was how silly and arrogant he sounded, or how happy the thought of carrying his child made her…but either way, Mellie's giggles were so strong and loud, she had to clamp her hand over her mouth to quiet them.

His growl told her he hadn't been expecting that particular reaction, and her giggles turned into a shriek when he suddenly rolled her over, reaching for the lacing of her gown.

"What are ye—?"

Her question was cut off when she gasped as he peeled

her gown off her shoulders, then reached for her leine and proceeded to quickly and efficiently disrobe her.

When he knelt between her thighs, still fully dressed, he grinned wickedly down at her. "Ye were saying, wife?"

The heat in his gaze was enough to fluster her, to make her completely forget whatever she'd been laughing about only a moment before. "I... Lachlan?"

He leaned forward, resting his weight on his hands on either side of her torso and lowering his lips to her breasts. With a moan, she arched off the mattress.

"What are ye doing?" she asked rather stupidly.

And then she felt his grin against her skin as his lips traveled lower, reaching her curls.

"I'm returning the favor."

And he did.

She was soon gasping for air, and any and all coherent thoughts were beyond her capability.

When her pleasure burst over her once more, she didn't bother silencing her cry.

It took a long moment before the room stopped spinning, and she could focus on his sly grin, but by that time, he'd already gathered her in his arms.

"I love ye, Mellie." He placed a kiss at the side of her head.

"I..." She took a deep breath, still having some trouble thinking. All she knew was, this man—this incredible man—was *hers*. They were married now, both of them finally getting the happy life which had been denied to them for so long.

He belonged to her, and she belonged to him; and here, in each other's arms, was exactly where they were supposed to be.

"Aye, my angel?"

She grinned up at him, impish and not at all uncertain.

She knew what she needed, what she wanted. What would make them both happy.

Forever.

"I think ye should get rid of yer clothes, *husband*, so I can show ye just how much I love ye."

His gaze turned molten. "Are ye ready to face the future with me, lass? To spend the rest of our days ensuring peace for our people, our clan, and our family?"

She knew, with absolute certainty… "I am ready."

AUTHOR'S NOTE ON HISTORICAL ACCURACY

Alright, listen. We've been over the inaccuracies of all our heroes wearing kilts, but there's a few other inaccuracies to address—or at least, things which might be hard to believe.

Okay, okay, stuff I made up.

First of all, let's address this "I am ready" line. Yep, that *is* the clan motto of the Frasers of Lovat (*"Je suis prest"* in French, because as you likely know, the Scots and French were closely connected via their hatred of the English). However, it's a little hard to believe that things like clan mottos, cries, and even colors were codified as early as 1320. The point is, some of these mottos are accurate, others are extrapolations.

By the way, the Frasers around Loch Ness are a separate clan from the Frasers in the Lowlands. In fact, in the 14th Century, the Frasers I'm writing about were a branch of the Lowland Frasers, even though their lands are extensive (all along the southern shore of Loch Ness).

Speaking of which, I'll bet you didn't expect to read a historical Scottish romance about Loch Ness which didn't involve the monster, did you? But it's hard to deny the tales of Nessie have been around for generations, so I *had* to at least reference her.

But that does lead me to another thing I made up: A Fraser stronghold at An Torr. The keep is named for a rocky outcropping near Dores/Durris, where I imagined Lachlan's beloved home to be.

Historically speaking, Lachlan and his brothers likely would have been born at Dounie Castle near the Beauly Firth or Inverness Castle on the Ness River. Both were important sites during the first War of Scottish Independence, so it's not unbelievable Michael Fraser would've moved his wife and sons to a smaller fortification. That would explain why Lachlan grew up at An Torr.

Speaking of Michael Fraser; I really gave him a bad name, didn't I? Luckily, he's completely made up…although I *did* base him heavily on Laird Simon Fraser (There are a half dozen Simon Frasers, just like all the John Comyns. So I named Lachlan's daughter Simone in homage). Laird Simon Fraser was a real person, and yes, he *did* support the Red Comyn for the throne. But he went on to save Robert the Bruce's life a few times in battle, and was ultimately drawn and quartered by the English as punishment. I've made Michael into a life-long supporter of the Comyn cause, and I hope the purists will forgive me.

You know who else is real? And whose story I *didn't* change? Isabel of Strathbogie, daughter of one Earl of Atholl, and sister of another. She was betrothed to Edward Bruce (who was King of Ireland!), Robert the Bruce's heir until his death. Edward sired her son, Alexander, who grew up to be the Earl of Carrick (Robert's family title before the whole becoming-a-king enterprise). But then Edward abandoned her to marry another (also named Isabel, which was convenient), but didn't sire anymore children.

The Crown's support of wee Alex (giving him lands and

AUTHOR'S NOTE ON HISTORICAL ACCURACY

his mother responsibility over them) showed that King Robert understood the lad was his closest male relative and thus heir…but who would back an illegitimate *nephew* as the next King?

Yes, between Edward's death in 1318 and Prince David's birth in 1324, there was no clear successor to the Scottish throne. Imagine the stress Queen Elizabeth must've felt, to bring a male child to term! We don't have exact dates of birth for her daughters Margaret and Maude, but we suspect there were also some pregnancies that did not result in living offspring. In between Robert's travels—through Scotland *and* Ireland—it was clear the royal couple was desperate for a male heir.

Which leads me to my last bit of historical inaccuracy: Scone. King Robert's main residence was Scone Abbey, which is often called a Palace (so that's what I called it, to avoid confusion about Elizabeth hanging around an Abbey). The structure they would've lived in has long since been replaced by the Palace which stands today. Which means I got to make up a bunch of stuff about what it might've looked like.

But Scone Palace (and the various alleyways around Scone!) will definitely be relevant in the last installation of this series.

What's that? You didn't think we were *done*, did you? There's still one Angel left, and you can bet Rosalind is going to fall hard when she finally comes face-to-face (or rather, lips to lips) with Lachlan's younger brother…the mysterious, and traitorous Cameron Fraser.

Is Cam the protective brother-figure Court remembers? The frightened lad Lachlan remembers? Or have his years as the leader of the Red Hand turned him into the villain the Angels suspect?

Keep reading for a sneak peak from ***The Thief's Angel***!

But first, I want to extend a personal invitation to join my reader group on Facebook. This is a fun, supportive community where we chat about romance novels, history, cute critters, and crafts. If you'd like a behind-the-scenes look into my stories, and want to help name some of my characters (Gillepatric was named thanks to a contest I ran in my Cohort!), then please do come hang out with us in Caroline's Cohort!

And now, for Cam and Rosa…

SNEAK PEEK

Rosa is the brains of the Angels, and isn't used to getting physical to subdue her suspects. But this particular suspect is going to get *very* physical indeed! Read on for a glimpse at **The Thief's Angel**, where Rosa and Cameron Fraser meet for the first time.

Movement at the head of the alley caught his attention, and he watched with some interest as a slight figure slipped around the corner, into the shadows. When she saw him, she hesitated, then stepped closer.

Another pick-pocket? Nay, this lass held herself close, her arms around her middle and her chin tucked against her chest, peeking at him from under lowered lashes. She was skinny and dark, her gown unlaced to show too much skin, and her skirts cut high enough to catch a man's interest.

A whore then, and not a particularly successful one, judging by her hesitation. She looked as if she expected him to lash out at her—likely had learned about men's tempers the hard way.

This is what Tess would grow up to be, if she didn't learn to fight back.

The dismal thought, so soon after his other depressing musings, had Cam sighing in pity. "Ye're new at this?" he asked the whore.

She started, her chin jerking up in what might've been a nod, before she huddled against herself and shuffled closer.

He sighed again. "Come here."

'Tis just my day for charity projects, I guess.

When she paused, he reached out and caught her elbow, gently tugging her closer. But he'd surprised her, and she stumbled into his arms. With a grunt, Cam caught her arms and settled her into the space between his legs, propping his arse against the wall behind him once more.

"Now, then, let's see ye…" he murmured.

When she didn't move, he tucked one finger under her chin and lifted her face. And sucked in a breath.

Saints above, she's lovely.

The lass had the small, delicate build of a songbird, or a fragile flower. Her skin was dark, her eyes darker still, and her black hair hung long and straight in a braid down her back. She watched him with those dark eyes wide, something not quite fear in her expression. Uncertainty?

Nay, she'd never attract customers like this.

Reaching over her shoulder, he pulled her braid forward, lying it across her chest. "Men like to imagine ye in bed, lass. They're no' going to pay money for someone all laced up prim and proper." Dropping his fingertip, he traced the upper swells of her breast. "Ye've made a good start, here, but ye must loosen yer hair if ye want to catch our attention."

The way she jerked at his touch, and the noise she made,

told him she wasn't yet comfortable in her new profession. Mayhap he could teach her to pick pockets instead...

Nay, ye cannae save them all.

"What's yer name, lass?"

Dark eyes flicked up to his, then settled on his chin. "Rosa," she whispered in a feather-light voice.

"Rosa," he breathed reverently, dragging his fingertip lower to the point where her shift parted to reveal the shadows between her breasts. The name fit her, a delicate petal amid the harshness of the world. "Loosen yer hair."

At his command, she took a deep breath and lifted her hands to her braid, fingers fumbling with the leather tie. She didn't meet his eyes as she made short work of combing out her hair, pulling it forward as if using it to cover her breasts.

He clucked his tongue, brushed her hands out of the way, and reached for her locks himself. It was smooth as water as it cascaded against his palm, and smelled faintly of roses.

That, more than the knowledge this woman was for sale, sent a jolt of desire straight to his cock.

"No' many whores smell as good as ye, Rosa," he murmured, shifting so she was further bracketed between his legs. "But ye need to learn to be bolder. Look me in the eye."

Dark lashes fluttered, but she did as he commanded, lifting her gaze from his chin to his eyes. He saw indecision in her expression, and offered her a quick grin. "Now tell me ye want me."

Her eyes grew wide. "My—milord?"

"Nay, donae call me that," he said with a shake of his head. It'd been many years since the title applied. "But calling a man *sir* will make his ego swell along with his cock. Try it."

Something flashed in her dark eyes, as if his words had changed something important. Her shoulders straightened and her chin rose. "Aye, *sir*."

His lips twitched. "Excellent. Now, ye have me pressed

against a wall, see? That puts ye in charge of the situation. Ye ken I have coin, because ye've seen my purse. Ye must make me believe ye want me. So what will ye do now?"

Before she had a chance to answer, Cam brushed her skin with his fingertips once more, liking the little shudder she gave. Had she been more experienced, he might've thought it feigned, but not *this* rose. His lips curling further, he dragged his hand across her chest, his palm settling around one breast, and squeezed just slightly.

She gasped and jerked away, before swaying back toward him. His smile grew as he brushed one thumb against the bud of her nipple, hard beneath the wool of her kirtle, and she gave a little moan. Her tits were as small as the rest of her, but filled his palm nicely.

Inside the trewes he wore, his cock jumped to attention.

What will ye do now?

The question hung between them, a challenged unanswered.

Until he dragged his thumb across her nipple again, and she moaned louder, then threw her arms around his neck and dragged his lips down to hers.

She looked like a rose, acted like a virgin, but she kissed like a woman who knew *exactly* what she wanted.

You can guess what Rosa is doing there in that alleyway, but after that kiss, her mission is going to change! Check out the rest of their story in ***The Thief's Angel***!

OTHER BOOKS BY CAROLINE LEE

Want the scoop on new books? Join Caroline's Cohort, an exclusive reader group! Or sign up for my mailing list by texting "Caroline" to 42828 to get started!

The Highland Angels
- *The Bruce's Angel*
- *The Highlander's Angel*
- *The Laird's Angel*
- *The Thief's Angel*

Steamy Scottish Historicals:
- *The Sinclair Hound*
- *The MacKenzie Regent*
- *The Sutherland Devil*
- *The MacLeod Pirate*

Sensual Historical Westerns:
- Black Aces (3 books)
- Sunset Valley (3 books)
- Everland Ever After (10 books)

The Sweet Cheyenne Quartet (6 books)

Sweet Contemporary Westerns
Quinn Valley Ranch (5 books)
River's End Ranch (13 books)

Click **here** to find a complete list of Caroline's books.

*Sign up for Caroline's Newsletter to receive exclusive content and freebies, as well as first dibs on her books! Or if newsletters aren't your thing, follow her on **Bookbub** for a quick, concise new release alert every time she publishes a book!*

Made in the USA
Coppell, TX
12 May 2021

55561552R10138